JAX

GUARDIAN GROUP SECURITY TEAM BOOK 3

BREE LIVINGSTON

Bree
Livingston
Publishing LLC

Jax: Guardian Group Security Team Book 3

Copyright © 2023 by **Bree Livingston**

Proofread by Krista R. Burdine

https://www.facebook.com/iamgrammaresque

Cover design by Book Covers for $30

http://www.facebook.com/stunningcovers

Bree Livingston

https://www.breelivingston.com

Publisher's Note: This is a work of fiction. Names, characters, places, and incidents are a product of the author's imagination. Locales and public names are sometimes used for atmospheric purposes. Any resemblance to actual people, living or dead, or to businesses, companies, events, institutions, or locales is completely coincidental.

Jax: Guardian Group Security Team Book 3 / Bree Livingston. -- 1st ed.

ISBN: 9798394973161

To my readers,

Thank you for cheering me on when I never thought I'd get this book written, much less published. You all seriously rock.

1

*R*iley Vance strained to hear the announcement that blared through the Bush Intercontinental Airport loudspeaker. In the distance, she could see puffy spring clouds floating by as a plane landed. She loved this time of year. Inwardly she giggled as the April 25th meme flitted through her mind. Funny, since today was that actual date, and it wasn't perfect by a long stretch.

She'd made it through security and decided it was best to roam the airport just in case her trick didn't work. Maybe if she stayed in the most crowded areas of the airport, she'd actually make it onto the plane alive. Not that she knew where she could go or who to trust, but she'd figured somewhere away from Houston would be a good start.

Before finding herself in Galen White's crosshairs,

she'd thought her luck was turning around after moving from North Dakota. At twenty-eight with no degree, finding an office job was like hunting for a jackalope, especially one that would pay enough to re-enroll in nursing school. No more overnights so she could properly study for tests, or weird schedules that she'd have to trade with other employees so she could make it to class.

For an entire year, she'd enjoyed weekends off, banker's hours, a medical plan, and a generous amount of paid time off. Sure, her boss had a bit of a slimy feel, but she'd been desperate, and after a little research on him, she'd taken the job. How bad could he be when he was supporting local women's shelters? She'd attributed the feeling she got to stress and the industry.

It had been fantastic until a couple of days ago when she got home and realized she'd forgotten her wristlet with her apartment key on it. All she'd planned to do was run into the front office, grab it, and go. Her quick in-and-out turned into a mission. The desktop she normally used was turned on, a micro flash drive with what looked like a dog tag chain attached was in one of the ports, and files were pulled up that she'd never seen before.

Of course, being a little miss nosey pants, she'd paused to read what was on the screen, and it'd led her down a rabbit hole of evil. It made her shiver to think that she'd been surrounded by that...disgusting stuff for a year without even a whiff that human trafficking was taking place. A shiver ran down her spine and she lowered her gaze to the floor, tugging her backpack tighter against her body.

With the seat of the office chair still warm, her heart had raced as she skimmed the files. Once she'd realized they were on the flash drive, she'd snatched it, hung it around her neck, and run straight from the warehouse to the police.

When she got there, though, she had a nagging feeling she needed to keep quiet about the flash drive, and her feeling was spot on once she was led into a detective's office. He was eager to take her information—until she spoke Galen White's name. The second it left her lips, the air was sucked out of the room and her skin tingled and itched. It couldn't have been more clear, she needed to find people she could trust.

She'd left the station and returned to her apartment building only to find two men milling around the entrance. After binge-watching *Hawaii Five-0* a few months earlier, she knew something was up and they were most likely looking for her. She'd sneaked as close as she could get to them and verified that her hunch was right when she overheard them discussing her keycode into the warehouse and the security alert it'd caused. She had been running from Galen's goons ever since.

Despite all her attempts to safely hide from them, they continued to find her. It became so frustrating that she'd phoned her mom, left a message, and then pitched her phone into a fountain after resetting it. In a desperate attempt to escape, she took a cab to a car rental company and used her credit card, then grabbed a different cab to the airport and paid cash for the first flight out of Houston to Las Vegas. Beyond that, her plan was unclear.

Riley's train of thought was interrupted as she collided with a solid surface. Startled, she took a step back and shook her head, only to realize that the obstacle was actually a person. She had been so deep in thought that she had unconsciously drifted closer to the entrance of the shops and accidentally bumped into someone.

"I'm so sorry I..." Her apology died on her lips as she lifted her gaze and found herself momentarily awestruck by the gorgeous man looking at her.

Whoa.

There was hot, and then there was this guy. Tall— well, taller than her which wasn't saying much—dark, wavy hair combed back, gorgeous dark eyes, square jaw, and a knee-weakening smile highlighting the most kissable lips she'd ever seen. With the way he was

4

dressed, in a button-up, slacks and loafers, it wasn't the biggest logical leap to suspect he was some sort of professional.

She was on the run from thugs, and there she was making a mental bullet list of all the man's appealing attributes as a wedding march played in the background. Apparently, she could multitask, just not when she was deep in thought and walking.

"You're good. Are you okay?" When she didn't respond, his eyebrows knitted together. "Hey, really, it's okay. Did you hurt yourself?"

Shaking her head, she pictured herself flipping on the light in her brain. "Oh, no. I mean, yes, yes, I'm... I'm fine." This man was short-circuiting her brain. Lava-hot embarrassment burned in her stomach and flared in her cheeks.

A light chuckle came from him. "At least now I know I'm not the only one who does that." The hint of a country accent made her insides gooey. Then his smile widened revealing dimples, taking him from hot to cute. Hot guys were hot, but cute guys? They were the ones a girl snuggled with and binged a favorite television show. That wedding march started playing again and she started humming just loud enough so that she couldn't hear it. She didn't have time to fantasize about the hottest guy she'd ever seen.

She palmed her cheeks with her hands to cool them

as a horde of butterflies took flight in her stomach. With the way she was acting, there was no doubt he was wondering if she'd sustained head trauma. "I'm really sorry, and yes, I promise I'm fine."

A voice came over the loudspeaker, and he glanced up to the ceiling as the man spoke. When the announcer stopped, he sighed. "Flight delay due to storm? Fantastic. There goes any chance I had of being on time."

Riley's shoulders sagged. Apparently, he was on the same flight she was and was equally bummed. Only she doubted that he had hired thugs hunting him down. She needed to get out of Houston before Galen's guys realized she'd pulled a car rental-plane switcheroo.

"You too, huh?" he asked.

Man, she really needed to work on her poker face, er, well, body. "Yeah."

A chuckle came from him, and he stuck out his hand. "Dr. Jax Kelly." He flashed her another brilliant smile.

Shaking his hand, she worked to ignore the little tingles skittering up her arm and replied, "Rrrriii... River Song." As soon as the name left her lips, she wanted to crawl into a hole. River Song as a fake name? What was wrong with her?

"Cool name. Never heard that one before."

Riley gave him a deadpan look. "You've never heard that name before?" Okay, she'd give him cute, but clearly, the man lacked any sort of cinematic taste whatsoever. How in the world was she supposed to snuggle him when he didn't know good television? His snack choices would probably be healthy too.

He shook his head. "Should I have? Are you famous? If you are, I'm sorry. I'm not very good at keeping up to date on the entertainment world."

And then it happened. She flat-out pig snorted. *Loudly.* She touched her fingers to her forehead, squeezing her eyes shut, begging the earth to just swallow her whole right then and there. She sighed. "If I could, I'd crawl into a hole and never come out." Or maybe a portal leading to the other side of the world. She'd be killing two birds with one stone. As far as plans went, it was fantastic.

"It'd be a tragedy for someone as attractive as you to disappear," he said, his voice dipping low. "As far as collisions go, a beautiful woman would easily be my favorite."

Her eyes popped open, and the intensity of his stare nearly made her giggle. Attractive? Beautiful? She was half tempted to look over her shoulder because he couldn't possibly be talking about her.

"Since we're both stuck here, would you want to join me for a late lunch? Maybe it'll help us pass the time." He paused and then added. "That is, if I'm under no threat of violence from a boyfriend or husband."

Boyfriend? Husband? Yeah, right. She worked to hold in a gut-busting belly laugh. "Nope, no threat there." Why on earth didn't she lie? Oh, she needed a good thump on the noggin.

As tempting as it was, she needed to pass on the opportunity. While working for Galan, she'd learned that he knew powerful people and he had friends everywhere, including doctors. She certainly couldn't trust her treacherous, twitterpated little heart at the moment, especially after the last guy she dated. Nope, she needed to turn herself around and get out of Mr. McDreamy's line of fire.

"I app…"

The sentence trailed off as two large men came into view. While she couldn't be positive they were there for her, they did have the same menacing look as the people she'd been running from… which meant, if she was right, the people who had been chasing her weren't the only ones. Dread pooled in her stomach as her gaze followed them. If they saw her…

As if reading her mind, Jax shifted, blocking her line of sight. "Is everything okay?"

She waved him off. "Oh yeah, everything's fine, I'm just…worried about a Mrs. Kelly beating me up." She patted herself on the back for the quick thinking and gave her best grin.

"Oh, no. I'm very single." Then something happened she couldn't or wouldn't have predicted, he blushed. As if he wasn't already adorable enough with the dimples and now this? Sheesh. "I mean, yes, I'm single."

Just as she resolved once again to decline his offer, the men strolled down the aisle again, stopped, and seemed to scan the area. Now what did she do? Put the nice guy in danger or try to keep herself alive so she could stop a monster?

Her stomach growled louder if that was even possible. "I speak stomach, and that was a solid yes."

Chuckling, he said, "Awesome. What sounds good?"

Something cheap? Talk about a needle in an airport haystack. As soon as she'd realized she'd been found out, and men were coming after her, she'd scrounged up all the money she could find—which wasn't a lot—and it needed to last until...well, she didn't know how long.

They ambled through the airport, in search of something that smelled enticing; with it being her pick, hopefully, she could choose one of the cheaper places. As they walked, she glance at him a couple times, wondering how it was possible he was still single.

"So, what do you do?" Jax asked.

How did she answer that? Anything and everything that paid the bills? "Uh, well, my last job, I was a secretary."

"Last job? Did you not like it?"

She'd loved it until she realized her boss was a trafficker and sent thugs after her. "I did, but we had a bit of a disagreement, and I quit."

"Oh, were you flying somewhere to interview or something?"

"I figured since I was between jobs, it was a good time to take a vacation and returned refreshed and ready to look for a new job."

"That's a good idea. Were you going to Las Vegas or were you catching a connecting flight?"

She gave a one-shoulder shrug. "Uh...I hadn't thought that far ahead." Truth. "I'm trying something new and being spontaneous." She held in a bark of laughter. She was a planner. A planner's planner. That's why she'd tried so hard to find a place to hide, so she could come up with a plan. She hated surprises.

"Guess that means I should hang out with you more. I hate surprises." He chuckled.

"You do? Meeeee... I like them when it comes to birthdays." She'd just told him she loved them and there her mouth was, tattling on her. Her brain needed to catch up.

He looked at her. "I don't even like birthday surprises. They've never worked out well for me, so I avoid them."

So, he was a doctor, he was cute, and he hated surprises. Box one, two, and three...check, check, check. Her heart squealed with glee. And it needed to put down the marker and step away from the boxes. There would be no more box-checking. How was she going to get away if her ADHD heart kept getting distracted?

There would be a meal and that was it. She squared her shoulders, resolving to focus on the mission. There were victims that needed saving and information that needed to get to the right people—perhaps the FBI—and that was all she needed to be concerned about. Relationships could come after this if she survived.

2

*a*s soon as Jax Kelly walked off the sky bridge into the Houston airport, the turmoil he'd been experiencing since the beginning of the year turned into a pool of frustration. He'd purposefully booked his flight to Las Vegas with a long layover so he could take care of some personal business.

It'd been a complete shock to learn that his dad had instructed a storage facility manager to contact Jax if something happened to him. Six months later, he was still dealing with the war between his head and his heart.

Shortly after his mom left, the man he'd considered his best friend had dropped him off at the babysitter's place and never returned. What on earth could the man have in storage that Jax would possibly want?

Now, thirty years later, here Jax was, paying the

rent on a storage unit that he should have just signed over to the facility; yet for some reason, he just wasn't able to do it. He'd had the same back-and-forth argument with himself each time he paid the rent.

He'd just ended his most recent call with the manager when his current gorgeous companion gave him a heel check. The woman was so attractive he'd nearly swallowed his tongue when he turned around. The first feature he noticed was her large, expressive brown eyes which stood out against her heart-shaped face and full, rosy lips. As his gaze swept over her, he noted long, silky-looking, honey-blonde hair that was neatly pulled back into a ponytail that fell several inches past her shoulders, and warm ivory skin complimented by a pink t-shirt and ankle-length jeans.

Jax inhaled as they passed a burger place and nearly salivated. He'd skipped breakfast and when he'd arrived in Houston earlier that morning, he hadn't been hungry. Now, he was famished. "How about here? It smells amazing."

After working for Guardian Group Security for so long, his instinct screamed she was in trouble, and he hoped that maybe he'd earn her trust enough to let him help. His spur of the moment invitation to join him for lunch had turned into something more when she began looking over her shoulder.

There was a chance that he'd jumped to the wrong

conclusion. If he was wrong, he'd happily board his flight to Las Vegas, Nevada, and attend the medical conference. Until then, he'd enjoy a meal with an attractive woman and hopefully keep his mind off his dad and the mysterious storage unit. Either way, it was a win-win for him.

"Oh, yeah, it smells delicious." She flashed a dazzling grin. "But I'm so hungry, I'm not sure I'm a good judge. Although, with as packed as it is, I'm guessing we're right."

They reached the hostess station, and after a short wait, they were seated at a booth near the back of the restaurant. In mere seconds, their waiter stopped at their table and took their drink orders.

River opened her menu and flicked her gaze to him. "So, you're a doctor? Medical or educational?"

"Medical. I'm an internist." If she was in trouble, he didn't want to scare her by talking about his employment with a security firm. He was a stranger and putting himself in her shoes, who was to say he wasn't one of the bad guys too.

"Oh. Do you have your own practice?"

In a way, he did. Yes, he worked for someone, but it was a private company where he treated individuals on a needed basis. "You could say that. I'm a concierge physician." It was a lie of omission, which he didn't feel great about, but it was better than an outright lie.

"That's interesting. I was in nursing school until recently."

A nurse? What were the odds? Then he realized she'd used past tense. "Was? Did you decide that wasn't the best field for you?"

Casting her gaze to the table, she shook her head. "No, I lost my job and had a hard time finding another one. I had to withdraw. I guess it's a good thing I hadn't had the chance to re-enroll yet."

"Hey, you'll get there one day." His heart took the information and began working on a white picket fence. Then his head yanked the hammer and nails away. Sheesh, the loneliness was getting to him. He needed to cool his jets.

She blinked hard and lowered her gaze to the table, using both hands to rub her eyes. "Sheesh. I thought contacts were supposed to be better, but they're awful."

He added another item to his list of reasons why he suspected she was in trouble. The visible marks on the bridge of her nose were pronounced enough that he'd taken note of them earlier. Add it to the excessive blinking, and it wasn't a shock to learn she was wearing contacts. Again, he'd keep that detail to himself. "When did you get them?"

Rubbing her eyes with her palms. "At my last eye exam, but when I tried them a few months ago, they bothered my eyes. Since I was going on vacation, I thought it'd be fun to go without my glasses. Boy, was I wrong."

"Oh, that's frustrating. Maybe start by wearing them for short periods of time and building it up until you grow accustomed to them."

Nodding, she puffed a piece of hair from her face and looked over her shoulder. "Would it gross you out if I switched here at the table?"

He flicked his gaze to the restaurant entrance. He'd kept watch too in case those two men he'd seen shortly after she ran into him, happened to show again. Chuckling, he pointed to himself, "Internist." He grinned. "That wouldn't even be close to the grossest thing I've seen, so go ahead."

Her cheeks turned the sweetest shade of pink he'd ever seen. "I guess you have seen a lot," she said as she picked up her backpack and dug through it. He waited while she switched out her contacts and dropped the case back in the bag. She closed her eyes, obviously trying to soothe them. "I'm not certain I can try those again. My eyes are so irritated."

"I'm sorry. On the bright side, glasses or no glasses, you're a knockout." Mentally, he checked himself. What was he doing flirting with her? If his Spidey senses were right, she was in trouble. Silence fell over them and lingered until it was awkward. He'd obviously opened his mouth and swallowed his shoe. "I'm sorry. I wasn't trying to make you uncomfortable."

A smile lifted her lips, and a blanket of pink covered her cheeks. "You didn't." A tiny giggle popped out. "It's just…no one has ever said that to me before and I didn't know what to say."

Talk about a crime. While she looked great either way, he found her even more alluring with the light pink framed glasses perched on her nose. "I find that hard to believe."

"Well, believe it. This nerd's got no game." She rolled her lips in as her face turned a brighter shade of pink.

"In my professional opinion, it's a fact that you're cute."

Her eyebrows hit her hairline. "Well, you're hotter than a frog in a boiling pot." She squeezed her eyes shut, palming her forehead. "I said that out loud, didn't I?"

Heat rushed up his neck to his ears. "Uh, yeah, and I can honestly say, I haven't heard that one before." Over the years he'd been called attractive, but that was a new one.

The initial attraction he had was growing exponentially. Beyond gorgeous and witty, she was incredibly likable. There was an easiness about her, and he had an instinct to trust her that he'd never felt before. Man, he hoped he was wrong about her being in trouble.

Not that it mattered. Even if she wasn't in trouble, the thoughts weren't something he needed to entertain. He was on-call, and with Noah's stringent hiring practices, it was proving difficult to find a second doctor. While he enjoyed what he did, it made relationships impossible.

He was happy for Tru and Hendrix, but their wedding had shined a light on the building loneliness he felt. Finding someone to love and share his life with had become a nagging desire that was getting harder to ignore.

With a groan, she straightened in her chair. "It's like my mouth has a mind of its own."

The deadly combination of attractiveness and wit was a magnet to him. "Seriously though, the glasses look great, but I can see them being a hassle, especially if they hurt."

With a shrug, she replied, "It could be worse." Sadness laced the words, and he resisted the urge to ask her why. She returned her attention to her menu. "I have no idea what to order."

While she was looking over the menu, she'd pulled out her wallet and rifled through it, sighing a few times. Just as she'd dropped it back into her backpack, the waiter returned with their drinks and took their order.

River smiled. "I think I'll have a side salad."

It was the cheapest thing on the menu, and even for a woman as petite as her, it wasn't enough food to leave her satisfied. He felt like a heel for not even considering she might not have the money to eat at an airport sit-down restaurant. He quickly scanned the menu, picked a couple of appetizers and the largest-sounding burger he could find with the hopes of convincing her to share as an unspoken apology for choosing such an expensive place without embarrassing her.

The waiter tapped on his tablet. "Order is in. I'll get it out to you soon."

Once he was gone, she lowered her gaze to the table. "Thank you."

"For what?" he asked, trying to feign innocence.

She looked up and caught his gaze. "You know exactly why. You ordered way more than you would ever be able to eat."

He shot her a sheepish grin. "That transparent, huh?"

"Like glass." She laughed, capturing her bottom lip with her teeth. "But very sweet." Her lips spread into the most breathtaking smile that reached her eyes. It was hands down her best smile yet. She was quickly moving him from the gorgeous to heart-pounding adorable. "Do you always go around rescuing broke damsels?"

Chuckling, he shook his head. "Just the pretty ones."

One eyebrow ticked upwards as her lips held the smile. "You, sir, are a charmer."

Whoa. Trouble or not, his ability to tamp down his interest in her was slipping. Perhaps he'd get the chance to sit next to her on the flight and get to know her better, and if things went well, he could extend his chance of spending more time with her.

It certainly wouldn't hurt to ask.

3

*R*iley plucked a stuffed mushroom from the basket sitting in the middle of the table, popped it in her mouth, and groaned. "These are so good, and I'm going to pop if I don't stop."

Just the pretty ones? There was a whole lot of holy in her guacamole.

A man as attractive as Jax was flirting with her? It was almost too good to be true. The thought made her pause. He was so charming and interesting and sweet. It made her wonder if he was sent to trick her into letting her guard down. She'd seen that in movies and television shows before. The big bad man sending an attractive minion to lure the gullible woman into a trap.

Except, that wasn't the feeling she got at all. Nothing about him was setting off any of her normal alarms. Granted, she was tired after two days of non-stop running, but even tired, she felt a sense of safety with him.

The cheapest thing on the menu was a side salad, and she was trying to make her money last. So that's what she picked. Then he'd done the sweetest thing ever and ordered extra food. She'd known the second he'd done it that he was doing it for her. He'd been too cute trying to feign ignorance. His eyes had sparkled when she'd busted him. How was the man still single and why, *oh why*, had she met him when she was trying to evade being caught by thugs?

Nodding, Jax smiled. "Yeah, it's pretty great for airport food." He took a sip of water and set the glass back down. "So, you said you wanted to be a nurse. Are you trying for a licensed practical nurse or are you doing something more involved?"

She'd asked herself that a multitude of times, waffling because of the added schooling she'd need and the balance it would take to work and study for anything beyond her LPN. "Uh, I don't know. I really liked the classes I was taking before I had to withdraw."

"I have a good feeling that you'll make a great nurse."

Narrowing her eyes, she grinned. "What makes you think that?"

He held her gaze until she gulped. "I just do. You have this calm air about you. I can see you taking a stressful, hard situation and making it easier to handle."

Good thing she was sitting down. "Uh, thank you. I think that's one of the nicest things anyone has ever told me."

His eyebrows knitted together like he was truly baffled. "That's surprising. I've enjoyed getting to know you."

If he kept up with the compliments, her cheeks were going to need medical treatment for third-degree burns. *Le sigh.* Her timing was awful. AWFUL! A sweet man, giving her compliments and buying her lunch. A sweet man who didn't deserve to be thrown in the middle of a situation that could get him hurt.

"Is your family supportive of your career? I think my mom will cry if I manage to get my LPN certification."

His gaze dipped to the table. "Uh, I don't know. I don't really talk to them."

She'd just determined that she felt safe with him, and now she was sure he'd lied. Well, maybe not totally, but it certainly wasn't the whole truth. They'd just met though, and family issues were hard. Why would he want to share anything so personal with a complete stranger. If she were honest, she didn't want to share much about her family either. "Oh. I'm sorry."

He lifted his gaze to hers, and her heart squeezed at the sheer amount of sadness coming from him. "It's okay. It's been a long time since I've seen them. How about you? You said your mom would be happy if you got your LPN certification."

"Thrilled is more like it." Yeah, the last thing he needed to know was what a loser she was compared to her siblings.

Over the next half hour, they picked at what was left of their meal and finished their drinks while they bounced questions back and forth. When the waiter finally dropped off the bill at the table, it was a subtle hint that the table was needed.

Once the bill was paid, they left the restaurant, stopped just outside and she could finally relate to that scene in Cinderella when the carriage turned back into a pumpkin and the night was over. Only, Riley's prince charming was a physician.

"Uh, did you maybe want to walk around while we wait for our flight?" asked Jax.

Oh, did she ever. While her heart screamed *do it*, like it was unaware of the danger she was in, her head planted its feet and gave her a firm *no*. She had to keep him away from Galen's radar.

She smiled as she worked to gather the courage to turn him down. "Uh, I wish I could, but I can't."

It was quick, but she didn't miss the downturn of his lips, making him look as disappointed as she felt. "Okay, well, then, I guess I see you when we board."

"Okay, see you then." She turned and it was an herculean feat not to take one last look. She mustered every ounce of resolve she had to keep walking.

If those men returned, she didn't want to chance them seeing her with Jax. Now that she thought about it, she hadn't seen them again since running into him. Perhaps they were just big dudes wandering through the airport. With their size, it was easy for them to stand out. She shook her head trying to clear it. This whole cloak-and-dagger thing was making her paranoid.

The thoughts rolled around in her head as she plodded through the airport, going from shop to shop, bored to tears, wishing with everything in her that she was still spending time with Jax.

As she strolled by a clothing store, a clearance rack stationed outside caught her attention. She pushed up her glass and began absentmindedly browsing the clothing on display until a sense of uneasiness settled around her. Her skin tingled. The hair on the back of her neck stood up, warning her of danger. Before she could react, she felt a sharp object forcefully pressed into her back, and a strong hand clamped around her right arm, immobilizing her.

"We are going to walk nice and slow out of here, got it?" His breath held the stench of a heavy smoker.

For a second, she pictured herself turning around and saying, *And what are you going to do if I don't?* Then her brain showed up just in time and made her think of all the people around her who could be hurt if she didn't go peacefully. She was trying to stop a monster, not become one herself.

"Move," the thug said, emphasizing it by pressing his gun harder into her back. Now sandwiched between two thugs, it was all she could do to keep her wits about her as they began walking.

Until now, her luck had held, and she'd been able to dart away at the last minute. As they passed security guards milling about, it almost seemed like they were choosing not to see what was happening. Surely, they saw the men holding her at gunpoint, and there was no way they couldn't see she was an unwilling captive.

In a way, she kind of understood. Maybe they had loved ones they were trying to protect or perhaps they didn't want to see the wrong that was being committed. It was much easier and safer to look the other way. If she'd done that, maybe she wouldn't be in her current predicament.

She nearly burst out laughing. There was no way

she could have done that. People were being hurt, and well, if she didn't make it out of this alive, then at least she was going with a clear conscience.

The man to her right pulled out his phone, tapped the screen, and his lips twisted into a sick smile. "Boss is eager to see you." His gaze raked from the top of her head to her toes. "Fresh face, sweet, big eyes."

Riley swallowed hard. She'd just figured they'd shoot her, but... bile rose in her throat as she now imagined something infinitely worse than dying. She had to get away from these men. Almost like he'd read her mind, the man fastened his meaty hand around her upper arm.

There had to be a way she could break free. The people Galen hurt—and was still hurting—needed her help. She let her body go limp, hoping it'd be enough to make the men let go. Instead, their grip tightened, and the one shoving the gun into her kidney, snarled as hefted her like a toddler to her feet. "Don't do it again. Boss didn't say we couldn't have a little fun before we got back."

These men weren't just evil...they were a step beyond, and her imagination was painting a picture that made her physically ill. She waited a couple of beats, jerked to a stop, and yanked her left arm free. "I need to use the restroom."

Right arm gun-guy leaned in again, getting so close

his nose was nearly touching hers. "Then hold it. Last warning. Do you hear me?"

Petrified didn't begin to describe her current state. She bit her bottom lip to keep it from trembling. No way was she going to give these men the satisfaction of seeing her cry. Not saying she wouldn't later, but she was going to hold it in as long as she could.

4

*J*ax hated that he was right. All the little cues had pointed to her being in trouble. He didn't know the specifics of her situation, but it was severe enough that two men had a tight grip on her arms while another held her at gunpoint, escorting her through the airport.

After finishing their meal, he'd hoped to keep the conversation going, but she'd turned him down. He'd understood. Her being a woman, it was wise to be cautious.

They'd parted ways, and he'd forced himself to let it go. He'd made it all the way to another terminal before the nagging feeling hit him so hard he couldn't shake it. He'd returned to their terminal, walked straight to the car rental kiosk, and rented a car.

Then he'd parked with a straight shot out of the

terminal in case he was correct. If they found themselves being chased, he didn't want to waste time bumbling through an airport parking garage looking for it. He'd debated a little on what to do with his luggage. Being stuck in Vegas without it didn't sound great, but in the end, he'd gone with his gut and left it in the trunk.

When he'd returned to the terminal, he'd checked through security again and scoured the place until he located her. If she didn't need his help, he'd end up with tired feet or possibly explaining himself to security if she caught him following her.

He would've called Ryder if he was certain she was in trouble, but he didn't want to pry into her business, especially if he was overthinking things. Right when he thought he'd overreacted, he saw those same two guys from before rushing towards her and knew he was right.

Moving as fast as possible, he ran to the nearest convenience store, grabbed a pair of socks, and loaded one with the heaviest objects he could find. He then threw down more than enough money to cover the cost before running out of the store, hoping to catch up with River.

Just as he was working on a course of action, she jerked them to a stop by yanking her arm free. She went from gorgeous to hot as she pointed her face up at the man with a gun and defiantly glared at him.

"I hear you," Jax barked as he swung the sock, catching the gun wielding man along the jaw. The gun flew from his hand and skittered nearly halfway across to the other side of the terminal. He then swung again and brought it down on top of the other guy's head like an axe. The man staggered back and fell.

Jax tossed the sock, watched it hit the man's midsection, and grabbed her hand. "We need to run."

Whatever internal debate she might have had, ended as one man stood. Her eyes went wide, and she grabbed Jax's hand. The second it was tightly secured in his, they took off.

Racing through the terminal, Jax frequently checked over his shoulder. It wasn't until he heard a loud scream that he realized why security wasn't following them. If the gun was the cause, there was also a good chance the two men would be slowed down too. They weaved through the crowds, running as fast as they could until they finally made it to the exit.

He held onto her hand as they ran across the pickup area to the garage and stopped at the car. He quickly opened the passenger door, pushed her inside, and rushed to the driver's side. He put the gear into reverse, narrowly avoiding a collision with another car.

"River, are you hurt?" He glanced at her. "River?"

Pushing her glasses up, she blinked a few times, shook her head, and replied, "No, I'm okay." She twisted in the seat, tilting her head. "Were you following me?"

"I asked you to eat with me, and you were about to say no. There were two intimidating-looking individuals who appeared to be looking for someone. You were wearing contacts instead of your glasses, and during our meal you kept looking over your shoulder." He gave a slight shrug. "It gave me the impression that you might be in danger, and I wanted to help."

"I thought you said you were a doctor." Her eyebrows knitted together. "How did you put all of that together?"

He glanced at her, lifted himself, and pulled out his wallet, handing it to her. "I am a doctor. I work as an on-call physician for Guardian Group, a private security firm out of North Carolina. I've picked up a few things while working there which is why I thought you were in danger." He pointed to his wallet. "That's my driver's license and the ID I use to enter the Guardian Group headquarters."

She opened the wallet, pulled out his ID, and stared at them for a few minutes. "How do I know these aren't fake?"

"Well, I guess you can't. I hadn't thought about

that." He *had* followed her. That was reason enough to be wary of him. "I don't know what else—"

His wallet slapped as she tossed it in the cup holder.

"You did buy me lunch and rescue me. That's at least enough to give you a little credibility." She crossed her arms over her chest. "What was in that sock?"

Good question. "Uh, I'm not entirely sure I could give you a complete list of things." He smiled. "I ran into the closest shop, and just grabbed anything I thought would be heavy enough to work. I'm sure the clerk is still scratching his head."

"I don't know what to say," she said, and faced forward. "I appreciate your help, but you don't know what you've gotten in the middle of. You need to drop me off somewhere and I'll figure out what to do from there."

He looked at her, taken aback. "Uh, no. There's no way I'm dropping you off somewhere and taking off. Those men were holding you at gunpoint. I'm a lot of things, but I'm not a coward."

"Jax…"

Out of the corner of his eye, he caught movement and checked the side mirror. A black SUV weaved through traffic, and now, followed them a few cars back. "Let me see if I can lose this guy."

River perked up, peeked around the seat, looked out the back window, and gasped. "I just don't know how they keep finding me."

It was possible there was a tracking device on her, but it was also possible for someone to have hacked into the airport security system. With as many cameras as they had, it would be easy to find someone. He knew Mia and Ryder well enough to know it was more than reasonable to suspect that.

"Have they been chasing you long?"

She faced forward and blew out a puff of air. "For about two days. I even tossed my phone in a fountain. I'd used my credit card to rent a car and then took cab to the airport. That's why I was watching my spending. I was trying not to use it all at once since it was all I had."

The SUV gained a little more ground and Jax punched the gas. "It's okay." He looked at her and smiled. "I didn't mind. Honestly, I'd really hoped I was wrong." He flicked his gaze from the rearview mirror to the side mirror. "Sheesh, these guys. I'm going to try to lose them in the side streets."

"Okay."

He eased the car over from the far left lane and took an exit. It felt more like an industrial area which he hoped would give him enough places to maybe hide for a second. Straining, he tried searching ahead for a spot and finally found what he thought was a good place to stop for a second. He slowed the car and took it down an alley way. Just as he breathed a sigh of relief, the back glass shattered, and River screamed.

As Jax hit the gas, the car's tires squealed, and it fishtailed. He worked to regain control of the vehicle, pulled out onto the street, and took the next exit. After an hour of driving through Houston in an attempt to escape his pursuers, he was lucky enough to spot train tracks and an incoming locomotive barreling toward the crossing. He held his breath as the car hit the incline and bounced over the tracks just as the crossing arm lowered, giving him the chance to get away.

The next time he cut the engine, he was in the garage of a safe house, grateful that he'd managed to get them both to safety. He raked both hands through his hair and as the garage door lowered, he relaxed.

His head dropped back on the headrest and let out a long exhale. "For a minute there…"

"Yeah," she said just above a whisper.

"River, are you okay?" He touched her arm and sat up. "Did you get hurt?"

"Not physically." She gave a nervous chuckle. "I think I'm mostly in shock. They shot at us. I mean, I know I was held at gunpoint, but…they shot at us. Just out in the open like it was no big deal."

Jax twisted in his seat to face her. Wide, fear-filled

eyes met his and there was no doubt she was in shock. "And it's okay to feel that way too. It's understandable to need a minute after all that."

Her bottom lip began to tremble. "Yeah…" The word came out so soft he almost didn't hear her.

"I'm sure all of this was terrifying. I promise you're safe, and I won't let anything happen to you, okay?"

Now her entire body was shaking, and tears were rolling down her face. If she'd let him, he'd make sure she was safe from whoever was trying to hurt her. For her sake, he hoped it was something simple, but with as determined as those men were, he had a sinking feeling it was more complicated than he could imagine.

5

*R*iley slowly opened her eyes and took a deep breath. A fruity scent hung in the air, and she realized she was on something comfortable and… she bolted upright, knocking her bookbag off the bed, her heart hammering against her ribs.

Those men had her at gunpoint and were taking her back to Galen. Jax had shown up, smacked them with a sock filled with something, grabbed her hand, and she'd made the snap decision to go with him.

She looked around the room. Clean with soft, soothing colors. By the light coming through the window, it was late evening if she had to guess.

A knock came from the door, and she grabbed her glasses, setting them on her face, and then picked up the lamp sitting on the nightstand. Sure, he'd shown her his ID, but just in case… "I'm awake."

"Are you dressed?"

Her eyebrows knitted together. "Uh, yeah."

Jax peeked in. "Sorry. I didn't just want to walk in on you." His gaze landed on the lamp, and he held his hands up. "You're free to go if you want. I promise I'm not going to hurt you."

Hanging her head, she set the lamp down and palmed the spot over her heart. If he'd really wanted to hurt her, it would have been easy to do while she was zonked out. "I'm sorry."

He stepped inside and remained by the door. "You have nothing to be sorry for. A strange man grabs your hand, and then you wake up in a strange place. I'd be grabbing a lamp too." He chuckled.

Still kind and gracious. She softened her posture and her shoulders rounded. "I think the last two days have frazzled me."

A smile lifted his lips, and when her eyes met his, all she could see was sincerity. "I gave you my identification earlier, but it was a little chaotic. If you want, you're welcome to see them again."

"I remember. You work for a security firm called Guardian Group. They're in North Carolina," she said softly.

"That's right." He stuffed his hands in his pockets. "They're great people. It was formed by Pamela Williams after her husband was murdered. To keep his memory alive, she'd formed the security firm to help people who had nowhere else to go or any to trust. River, you can trust us, and if you're in trouble, we can help."

Oh yeah, she'd given him a false name. Did she fess up? He *had* swooped in and rescued her from two men who were going to hurt her, brought her somewhere safe, and he'd kept a respectable distance. Granted, there was a chance he was trying to lull her into a false sense of security, but the same feeling of safety she had in the airport remained. "My name is actually Riley Vance."

Grinning, he nodded. "Well, I suspected it might be based on the way you reacted." He chuckled. "I still don't know who River Song is. I was being honest when I said I don't keep up with entertainment stuff."

Oh, she remembered that. He definitely needed an introduction to *Dr. Who.* "It's okay."

"If you're wondering, this is a safe house that my employer keeps. There are toiletries in the bathroom, and clean clothes in the closet. If you'd like to freshen up, you're more than welcome to."

A shower? Clean clothes? He was speaking her language. "That'd be nice."

"Okay. Once you're finished, if you'd like, we can call my boss and talk to him. If we can, we'll be more than happy to assist, okay?"

Now she was in a quandary. They didn't know who she was running from, and as bad guys went, Galen White was beyond bad. On the other hand, they were a private security firm. Maybe they'd know people trustworthy enough to have the information she had.

"I tell you what. Think about it. I'll heat up some water and make you some tea. You can let me know then." He smiled, pulled his cell phone from his pocket, and set it on the table closest to the door. "Feel free to use that too. Okay?"

Nodding, she returned his smile. "Thank you."

He shot her one last lopsided smile and stepped out of the room, shutting the door behind him. She flopped back on the bed, thanking whatever brought him into her path. It'd been days since she felt any sort of security, and the thought of maybe getting some help did appeal to her.

She stood, walked to the table, and picked up his phone. Part of her wanted to text her mom and the other didn't want to make her worry. They maybe spoke once every other month. More than one text in a week would alarm her, and twice in one day would mean the national guard would be looking for her.

Instead of texting her mom, she shuffled to the bathroom. The colors matched the bedroom, and the counter was lined with all sorts of body wash, shampoos and conditioners, and lotions. It almost reminded her of a department store.

An hour later, she felt human again. She'd washed off the ick she'd accumulated the last few days. It'd given her time to make a decision. If the Guardian Group could help, she was going to take them up on it.

Toweling her hair dry, she put on her glasses, left the bedroom, sauntered down the hall, and stopped when she reached the open concept living room slash kitchen with adjoining dinette.

Jax glanced over his shoulder and smiled. "Are you feeling any better?"

"Uh, maybe? The shower helped a ton." She set his phone on the counter. "Thank you."

"Sure." He turned his attention back to the kettle on the stove. "I'll have hot chocolate ready as soon as the water boils. I looked for tea, and I guess it wasn't restocked after the last person stayed here. So, I hope you find chocolate soothing."

"Chocolate in all forms is considered soothing." She chuckled.

The kettle went off, and he filled the mug he had on the counter. As he stirred it, he glanced over his shoulder. "Have you decided what you'd like to do? As much as it would pain me, you're free to go if that's what you want."

When she didn't respond, he handed her the mug

and leaned his hip against the counter. "I know I'm asking a lot when it comes to trusting me, but..." He sighed and shrugged. "I've really got nothing beyond that. I promise I'm a good guy."

Sheesh he was cute. "Actually, I really would like the help."

A long sigh poured out of him like he was holding his breath while he waited for her to answer. "I was hoping you'd say that." He grabbed his phone and waved his hand toward the table. "We can sit there."

Following him, she set her mug down and took a seat while he set his phone in the middle of the table, tapped the screen, and put it on speaker.

"Jax?" A man answered.

"Hey, Noah."

"Shouldn't you be at the conference?"

Now she felt like a heel. She'd completely forgot about his conference which he was missing because he'd helped her.

Jax grinned as he looked at her. "Well, I've had a bit of a detour."

It took effort to hold in the laughter. Detour. Talk about a polite way to describe a messy situation.

"What sort of detour?" Noah asked.

"I met someone at the Houston airport, and I think she could use our help."

Noah chuckled. "Okay. Does she want our help?"

Jax looked at her and waited. Wow. This was a new experience. Her ex would talk over her, yet here Jax was letting her speak for herself.

She nodded. "Yes, I would. I don't know who to trust or where to go."

Papers rustled in the background. "Would you be okay if I turned this into a video call?" Noah cleared his throat. "That way you've got eyes on me."

Again, Jax waited. Boy did she like that.

"That's fine." At this point, she'd eat used gum before she'd believe they were bad guys, and that was saying something since she couldn't even watch *Elf* without gagging.

Pulling the salt and pepper shaker closer, he leaned his phone against them as a video call came through and he answered it.

Whoa. This guy was gorgeous too. Shaggy brown hair, blue eyes, and built like a tank. He was a stark contrast to Jax's slim physique. "Hello, I'm Noah Wolf with Guardian Group Private Security Firm. If you don't mind, I'll be taking notes while we go over your situation. At the end, we can discuss options and go from there. Does that sound okay?"

"That's fine."

"Okay, like I said, start from the beginning with as much detail as you can recall, even if it seems inconsequential. Little details can mean more than you think sometimes." He smiled.

Riley sucked in a lungful of air and started at the beginning, giving Jax and Noah the full rundown of what she'd seen on the computer until she'd run into Jax, literally. Again, she held back the flash drive. For some reason, each time she tried to divulge it, she couldn't. If that information didn't get to the right people, everything she'd been through would have been for nothing.

"How long were you working for the shipping company?"

"A year. It seemed like the perfect job at the time. Mr. White seemed a lit—"

Noah's head jerked up with his eyebrows drawn together. "Wait. Would his first name be Galen?"

Riley sat back, finding herself more than a little stunned. "Uh, yeah. Galen White." How did a security firm out of North Carolina know who he was? While he was fairly well known in Houston, she wasn't aware that his reputation extended all the way to the coast. "He's the owner of Exotic Lands Imports and Cargo Limited."

Noah leaned to the side a little, like someone would when they were wanting to get someone's attention from across the room. It seemed like his efforts were fruitless when he finally called out a woman's name. A few seconds later, she joined him in front of the camera.

Noah said, "Riley, I'd like you to meet my wife and partner."

Her smile reached her eyes. "Hi, I'm Mia Wolf. It's nice to meet you."

"She's been working for Galen White the last year."

The smile slipped and her gaze flicked from Riley to Noah and back. "Galen White?" Her lips twisted into a sneer. "That man is pure evil."

Well, that went a long way toward building trust, but that flash drive was hard proof. Riley needed more than a few disgusted looks to fork that drive over.

Noah worked his jaw and exchanged a look with Mia, returning his attention to Riley. "We've spent the last decade trying to bring that man to justice. He has committed unspeakable crimes. He doesn't just need to be in prison, he needs to be buried under it." Venom laced the words.

Mia nodded in agreement. "Riley, you are in an enormous amount of danger. You've stumbled into something that reaches well beyond Houston."

Dread pooled in Riley's stomach. Danger held an ominous tone with the way she spoke it.

Jax swept his gaze from Riley to the screen. "Is this the guy who worked with Tom Harrison? I thought he was small time."

Nodding, Noah replied, "He was, but with Tom's death, there was a void. Galen stepped in and happily took his place. He's ruthless. He makes Tom look tame."

Mia sat forward, her gaze connecting with the camera. "This man has a lot of connections. He has friends in high places, deep pockets, and his claws into more organizations than I can list. He's used black hats to silence anyone or anything that might threaten him or his power."

"I know about some of his connections. He's got an award gala in about a week. He'll be accepting a life-time achievement medal from a women's domestic abuse charity." It made her shudder just thinking about it. Places that were supposed to be trustworthy were being invaded by wolves in sheep's clothing.

Closing her eyes, Mia seemed to force back what-ever emotions hit her. She opened her eyes and pinched her lips together. "You have information, and he will do everything in his power to make sure it never goes anywhere."

"Do you have any family, Riley?" Noah asked.

She nodded. "My mom, dad, and siblings. They're all over the place though. I mean, I love them, but we're not super close."

"Okay. I'll need names and locations. You can text those to me. We have secure communications here, so we'll get in touch with them after we hang up." His lips turned down. "Anyone else?"

For a second, she thought about Charlie, her ex, but she'd ended that before arriving in Houston. Shaking her head, she replied, "No."

"Are you still in Houston?" Noah directed the question to Jax.

"Yeah, I rented a car, grabbed Riley, and once I was sure we weren't being followed anymore, I brought us to one of the safe houses."

Noah scrubbed his hands with his face. "It sickens me to say this Jax, but you two are on your own. We have no idea who to trust, especially in Houston. He has a network that stretches across the country, and technology is the enemy here. He probably already knows who you are, and that you work for Guardian Group."

Riley's heart hit the floor. She'd had no idea what she was doing when she decided to grab that flash drive. Not that she would have done anything different, but it would have been nice to know the risks. Plus, Jax had walked in like a knight in shining armor, and now he was in danger because of her too. She turned to Jax. "You need to drop me off somewhere and—"

Shaking his head, he crossed his arms over his chest. "No, you're stuck with me at this point."

Mia nodded. "Jax is right, and when Galen finds out who he works for, he'll be coming just as hard, if not harder, for Jax. At this point, you need to stick together, stay safe, and do whatever you have to get out of Houston." She took a deep breath and continued. "Ryder and I are two of the best, and more than once they've bested us. They're nasty, immoral, unethical people. They'll work for anyone as long as the pay is high enough. You need to ditch all of your electronics. If it's possible, find an older vehicle that can't be tracked. By the end of the day, there'll no doubt be a law enforcement BOLO sent out to all three major routes into North Carolina, so you'll need to stick to back roads."

Color had drained from Jax's face, and he looked as scared as she felt. It was almost like the severity of the situation was finally hitting and she felt even worse now that she'd eaten lunch with him.

As if reading her mind, he looked at her and covered her hand with his. "I know this is overwhelming, but you have my word I'll get you to safety."

Noah exhaled heavily. "Stay away from the coast, especially. No credit cards. Take all of the cash that's in the safe. Get a burner phone. Don't use it unless necessary. Stay under the radar. Once we end this call, reset your phone and destroy it." Noah looked from Jax to

Riley and back. "We'll see you when you get here, okay?"

"Yeah, we'll see you."

Jax ended the call, pulled up Noah's number, and handed the phone to Riley. "As soon as you finish texting the names of your family, I'll wipe it. While you're doing that, I'll grab a few things and we'll head out."

Overwhelmed didn't begin to explain how she felt. She'd known what Galen was doing was evil, but she'd had no idea of the scope. It felt like the world had waddled onto her shoulder and parked itself like a parrot.

Jax set a finger under her chin, lifting her head until his gaze locked with hers. "I will do everything in my power to get you to safety, and I will die before I let anyone get their hands on you. You have my word on that, and I don't break my promises." The words held a level of conviction she'd never experienced before.

Nodding, she gave him a small smile. "I believe you." Surprisingly, the thought of him dying squeezed her chest to the point of aching.

His lips quirked into a smile. "All right. Time to get moving."

Riley flicked her gaze skyward, praying that whoever might be listening would guide their feet and keep them safe, especially Jax. He'd jumped in with both feet, and now he was swimming in the pool of piranhas with her.

He pledged to keep her from harm. Silently, she made the same pledge to him. Maybe between the two of them, they'd actually make it to North Carolina in one piece.

6

*S*itting at the storage facility, Jax's emotions were in a freefall and his heart ached. He'd made a promise to Riley to get her to North Carolina safe, but it was like he was kicked in the chest by a mule.

If it weren't for the fact that he had a feeling his dad's storage unit was full of things they might be able to use, they would already be out of the city. Before his dad had dumped him, they'd often gone camping, hunting, and fishing. It was their thing, and yet, his chest continued to constrict.

Noah and Mia had spoken of Tom Harrison before, and Jax knew the guy was scum. He hadn't elicited the fear he saw in Noah and Mia's eyes. Which meant there wasn't time to delve into his childhood trauma.

"Are you okay?" Riley laid her hand on his arm. "I'm so sorry I got you into—"

There was no way he was dumping his sob story on her. Very few people knew about his dad, and two of the names on that list were Noah and Mia. The last person rounding it out was Ryder's wife, Kennedy. She'd helped Ryder with his PTSD and she was the only therapist Jax trusted enough to even consider talking about his dad ditching him and landing in foster care.

He looked at her. "It's not that, I promise. I've needed to do this for months, but I'd been putting it off." He visualized himself setting the mental tornado aside and smiled. "Come on. We'll get the key and with a little luck, we might find a few things we need before searching for a car."

Once Jax had the key, they drove to the unit that the manager had shown him on the map. The thing was huge, and Jax couldn't for the life of him imagine what his dad could possibly need with a fifteen hundred square foot unit with a roll up garage door.

He parked in front, cut the engine, and stepped outside. Tinges of pain radiated from his heart down through his arms. If he wasn't a doctor, he'd be wondering if he was on the verge of having a heart attack. He honestly thought he'd put his childhood behind him, but getting that phone call had made it abundantly clear it wasn't. The anger, fear, confusion, and pain... it was still just as raw and real as it was the last time he saw his dad drive away.

Taking a deep breath, he stuck the key into the lock, and his stomach did a somersault. He set his forehead against the cool steel, fighting the urge to run. It was pathetic. Riley was counting on him and here he was having a panic attack over things that happened thirty years ago.

He needed to snap out of it, but it was like the memories were wrapped around his throat, squeezing the air out of him. Slender fingers tangled with his and then tightened, as if she was trying to infuse him with strength.

With his head still on the door, he looked at her. "Hopefully, this doesn't make—"

She held up her hand, stopping him. "Whatever you were going to say, the answer is no. You saved my life. Your knighthood is firmly intact." She smiled.

A light breeze picked up her hair, making her tuck it behind her ears. He'd liked it when it was up, and even more so now that it was down. It was much longer than he'd thought. Man, what he wouldn't give to run his fingers through it. Seriously, what was his problem? There was a location and time problem and his focus needed to be squarely on getting her out of Houston.

With one more deep inhale, Jax opened the unit, flipped on the lights, and sucked in a sharp breath as his dad's old '74 Dodge Power Wagon pickup and camper they'd used… "I can't believe it." Both looked as though they'd been completely restored. That is, if the interiors matched the shiny exteriors. The Wagon had the look of being restored while a clear coat over the patina gave it character, and the camper was a showroom piece.

To the right there was a table with tools for making flyfishing lures, and a large gun cabinet with a few shotguns, most likely a couple of 12 gauges and a 16 gauge, butted against the table. If his dad did things like Jax remembered, there'd be enough ammo in the bottom of the gun cabinet to take out a herd of deer.

This storage unit might actually hold tools to help them make it to their destination.

Riley let go of his hand and looked around. "This is really cool."

Jax absentmindedly nodded. It was beyond cool. His dad had left him, forcing Jax into the foster system and eventually a group home. Yet here he was… making fishing lures and camping? Jax's ability to hold in what he was feeling was diminishing by the minute.

If he was going to get Riley to safety, he'd have to deal with this later. Otherwise, he was going to drown, and they didn't have time for that. He forcefully pushed the thoughts away. "Come on, we need to get going."

The camper would be staying. He'd checked it out, and the interior was incomplete. As far as attention grabbing, he was already worried about the pickup. Adding the camper would make them stick out even more.

After loading the truck up with camping equipment, a shotgun—

surprisingly enough, his dad even had a 9mm—and ammo, he pulled it out of the unit, and then drove the rental car inside. He'd completely forgotten about it, so before he wiped his phone, he'd sent Noah a quick text letting him know about it and the information for the storage unit so that the rental company didn't put out an alert that it was stolen.

When they neared the gate, Jax rolled to a stop. "We've got cameras." He tugged the baseball hat he'd put on a little lower. It was dark, and by the looks of the feed in the office, the picture would have been grainy. He still wasn't taking the chance. A few miles down the road, Jax finally felt like he could relax a little.

Riley ran her hand over the seat cushion and across the dash. "I know we're in mortal danger, but this truck is so cool."

Grunting a laugh, he took a quick glance around. "Yeah, it's rocking the red interior isn't it."

She laughed. "Yeah, it really is, but man these old trucks are neat." She continued to look around, running her hand over the arm rest and checking out the visor. "I love old cars and trucks."

His chest tightened, thinking about the times that he and his dad had gone camping. Before...his world was turned upside down. He needed to get himself in check and stay focused. Yeah, he'd had it hard as a kid, but the woman sitting next to him needed his attention as well as the people being hurt by Galen. This just wasn't the time to deal with it.

Riley twisted in her seat. "I wish I hadn't dragged you into this. I feel so guilty."

"I'm glad you did. Those men would have hurt you, and Galen White needs to go down. If he's worse than Tom Harrison, Noah's right, he should be buried under the prison." He smiled as he gave her a quick glance.

"I actually feel like I can breathe again."

"How did you manage to outrun him?"

A giggle popped out. "I'm barely taller than a leprechaun. You'd be amazed at the places I can hide."

He belly-laughed at the image it conjured. "Okay, I'll give you that you're short, but you're taller than that."

Nodding, she smiled wider. "Not by much, and I used it to my advantage. Doghouses, clothing racks in a clothing store, and so many other places. They'd find me though, and I had no idea how until it dawned on me that they were using my phone."

"They're good at what they do. That's why they've evaded getting caught before now. What you did that night is probably one of the most courageous things I've ever heard. You walked into a lion's den filled with lions without hesitation."

Riley scoffed. "I had no idea what I was walking into that night. Had I known…"

"You would have made the same choice." With what he saw in the airport, the way she handled herself, she was brave. "You saw a chance to make a difference, and you stepped up. That takes a level of bravery most don't have." When Jax looked at her, her lips were quirked in a smile and her cheeks were flame red. "You're really cute when you blush too."

She ducked her head, but he caught the tint of her cheeks turn up a few more shades. "You're just being nice because—"

"I'm not that nice of a guy."

Narrowing her eyes, she lifted an eyebrow. "You are the nicest guy, and you want to talk about brave. I didn't know what I was getting into. You did and still chose to stick with me." She paused a moment and it felt like she wasn't just talking about their current situation. "Most people wouldn't have done that."

In Jax's mind, he was doing exactly what anyone else would have done. She was in trouble. He could help. Long before Guardian Group, he'd held that philosophy. That was part of what drew him to them. Noah, Mia, Ryder, Tru, Hendrix...all of them were people who would risk themselves for others. It was the right thing to do when someone was in trouble, or an injustice needed to be righted.

"Still, thank you."

He appreciated the gesture, but he didn't know what to say. *You're welcome* sounded weird to him, even if it was the way people typically responded. What little he knew about her, he liked, and the idea of her facing down Galen alone tugged at his heart.

Silence settled over them for a moment. "Do you think Galen will try to hurt my family?"

Man, he wasn't sure how to answer that. "I'll be honest. He might. It would be the best way to gain leverage over you. The thing is, even if you surrendered yourself, there's no guarantee he wouldn't hurt you and your family, especially if he gets his hands on them. They'll be a liability at that point."

"Oh." The word came out almost too soft to hear it. "Do you think we'll have to go into witness protection?"

That wasn't just a hard question, it was ugly, and he wasn't sure he'd like the answer. "I don't know. If I'd had my head on straight, I would have asked Noah and Mia." He paused. "Maybe? It'll largely depend on how safe you are once we get your information to the right people. That program isn't nearly as easy to get into as people make it out to be. There are a lot of restrictions. Ultimately, it'll be your choice."

"Okay." She took a deep breath. "This is so overwhelming."

Nodding, he glanced at her. "I'm sure it is. It's a lot to think about. You're not alone though. For now, it's me and you against the world."

The last line squeezed his heart. It's what his dad would say when they'd head out on a trip, only he'd learned the hard way that he was on his own. If he concentrated a little too long, he could still feel the ache when the social worker showed up. He wasn't going to do that to anyone else. Once he was in, he was in.

He was getting Riley to safety or he'd die trying.

7

*Y*awning, Riley stretched awake. "Oh, no, I conked out on you. I'm so sorry."

The last thing she'd seen was the "Leaving Houston" sign. The tension in the cab had frayed her nerves as they'd driven through the city, on the edge of their seats, trying to make sure they weren't being followed. Every dark sedan or SUV gave her anxiety. As soon as the city was in the rearview mirror, the adrenaline had turned to relief and then exhaustion.

Jax waved her off. "Nah, don't be. You probably needed it after all you've been through."

Well, she wouldn't argue with that. Truth be told, she could use more. "How long did I sleep?"

She tried to make out the scenery as he drove, but to say it was pitch black was an understatement. In

Houston, taking a taxi far enough away to leave the city lights behind, was out of her budget.

One of the things she liked about her small North Dakota hometown was the ability to see the stars at night. She took her glasses off and cleaned the smudges that her cheeks had made. It'd been a while since she'd seen such a glittery display of stars.

"We crossed into Arkansas a little while ago. I figured I'd let you sleep, and we'd stop somewhere for a bathroom break and pick up a map while we're there."

Now that he mentioned it… "Yeah, the bathroom break sounds awesome."

He chuckled. "I thought it might." He cleared his throat. "When we get there, stick close to me. I've got a couple of fishing hats in the back seat, so we can use those to cover our faces. If anyone looks suspicious, tell me. Part of keeping you safe is working together. Okay?"

"Okay, I can do that."

Silence fell over the cab as she tried to think of something, anything to maybe chat about. Questions posed a threat level though. If she asked him questions, it would only be fair for him to do the same. Just how much did she want him to know? What if he realized she wasn't worth knowing?

There was part of her aching to ask about his dad.

The depth of sadness she felt coming from him had made her heart hurt. The way he'd leaned his forehead against the door of the storage unit, and the deep breaths he'd taken. In a lame attempt to give comfort, she'd held his hand. It was the very least she could do after he'd come to her rescue.

He'd stepped inside, turned the lights on, and gasped. By the way he looked around, he was in total shock. But as much as she wanted to dive deep into Jax, it wasn't the right time. He didn't know her, and if he did eventually tell her, it needed to be in his own time.

What she really wanted was her phone. It wasn't until she'd tossed it that she realized how much she relied on it. Before that, she would have laughed off the idea that she depended on it too much. Now, there were no distractions from the awkward, painful silence eating at her.

It was dark, they were practically strangers, and if this lasted the entire way to North Carolina, she'd be batty. Maybe if she kept the conversation light, she could avoid probing questions. She twisted in the seat, leaning her back against the door. "So, since we're in this together, maybe we could get to know each other?"

"Okay. You start."

Yeah, she'd expected that, but it would have been a

nice surprise if he'd gone first. "What do you do for fun when you aren't on call?" she asked, taking her glasses off and setting them on her lap, giving her nose a break.

He sank further into the seat. "Uh, well, it's hard to commit to things because of being on-call. I was a skateboarder when I was a kid, and I'll do that sometimes. Mostly, I read a lot." He paused a moment. "How about you?"

"Studying." She chuckled. "I'm only half kidding. Nursing school wasn't hard, but I didn't just want to pass the classes, I wanted to be the best nurse I could be."

If she concentrated on it too hard, she'd cry. She'd worked for Galen and saved as much as she could so she could re-enroll in school. Classes were starting in the summer, and she'd planned to register. Would witness protection let her go to nursing school?

"I remember those days studying." He whistled. "Man, it'd be impossible to count the hours I spent with my face in a book. I felt the same way you do though. I didn't just want to be a doctor. I wanted to be the best doctor."

For some reason, that didn't surprise her. "What medical school did you attend?"

"John Hopkins. The Navy paid for it."

A picture of him in dress blues was as clear as the

sliver of moon in the sky. *Great.* Now she'd spend the remainder of the trek being teased by that image. He was hot-ta-ta-ta and in a uniform, it'd be like taking a stroll on the surface of the sun.

"Did you start working with Guardian Group right after that?"

He shook his head. "No. Right after I turned thirty, I left the military and joined Doctors Without Borders. After a few years with them, I met Noah. I've been there ever since."

Holy wow. "And how old are you?"

His laugh was deep and rich. "I'm thirty-six." He paused and then added. "I worked hard in high school and college. When I say I understand about studying, I mean it. That's literally all I did. I had my license by the time I was twenty-nine."

Whoa. So, he wasn't just gorgeous and kind, he was also wickedly driven and smart. "That's quite the accomplishment. All I've got is a high school diploma and a dream of one day finishing nursing school. Hope that doesn't make you think less of me."

"Why would it?"

She often avoided telling people that because of the way they'd look at her afterward. "Because the people I meet do care about that. When I tell someone I don't have a college degree, and they find out I dropped out of nursing school, their opinion of me goes even lower." Even her family would have that disappointed look sometimes. She didn't think they were trying to be mean. They were all so accomplished, and they didn't understand why she wasn't as well.

"I don't value people based on their education. I value people by the content of their hearts, character, and strength. I'd say you're aces in all three categories."

Riley palmed her cheeks trying to cool them. How had she been so fortunate to run into a great guy like him? Whoever had a hand in that would have her eternal gratitude. Then she gave the unknown entity the stink eye as *witness protection* waved in front of her eyes. Talk about lousy timing.

"So, what made you decide to be an internist?"

A pregnant pause had her wondering if he'd answer.

"Jax, I won't push. Just know that whatever you tell me will never, ever go anywhere else. You saved my life, and being a good listener is really all I have to offer in return."

He took a deep, shuddering breath. Finally, he replied, "I… thank you, I just can't. Not yet."

"I understand. The offer has no expiration date either." She rolled her lips in, looking for a new direction, and asked, "What's your favorite book?"

The breath he let out felt more like a thank you than a simple sigh. "Wow. Hard question. I read a wide variety of things. I'm not sure I can pick just one. I've read most of the classics, *Lord of the Flies*, *Scarlet Letter*, *Wuthering Heights*, and the list goes on. Out of them, my favorite is *The Picture of Dorian Gray*. As for contemporary books, there are quite a few, and there's no way to pick a favorite. I've read several medical studies to keep up to date on new findings and current research." He leaned his head against the headrest. "Do you like to read?"

"Depends on the season I'm in. Sometimes, I'm ravenous and can't get enough and others, I can't get past the first sentence, even on a book that I've read in the past and loved. I'm a movie and popcorn girl."

He grunted a laugh. "The last movie I saw was Dr. Zhivago, and that was in high school when I didn't have a choice."

Her jaw dropped. No movies? "Really?"

Chuckling, he nodded. "Really. I just never got into them. The same with television."

No movies. No television. She was quickly running out of things she could have in common with him. "I've never met anyone who didn't love at least one or the other."

"Eh," he said and shrugged. "If I met someone who enjoyed those things, I'd watch with them. For me, it'd be less about the movie or show, and more about spending time with them."

Jax sure was different than Charlie. Her ex loved movies and stuff too. Only he never wanted to watch what she did. He liked B-movie horror, and she hated it. Two hours of chainsaws and nearly naked women just didn't appeal to her. It was bad enough that they'd find other things to do when he was in town.

"I feel that way too. If I met someone that—just for example—loved reading, I'd offer to go to the bookstore, find a book we both liked and read it."

He gave a small shrug. "To me, that's what makes a relationship. Compromising and looking at things from their perspective. I think a good relationship is putting the other person ahead of yourself. I'm not saying at the expense of your own happiness, just that you think about them when you're making choices. They're your partner."

It was a good thing it was dark; otherwise, he'd see the goosebumps that had broken out all over her. She didn't have to think too hard to see being in a relationship with him. "Me too. Although, I don't think I could have said it as well as you did. I want to support the person I fall in love with, and I want them to want to support me."

"Exactly. I think a relationship is a decision. Feelings have a way of misleading us. At the end of the day, it's the head telling the heart, I love and want this person, get on the train. And then not giving it the option to choose the station."

"Are you from the area around John Hopkins?"

"No, I'm from Mississippi." The dash gave off just enough light she could see him glance at her. "Jackson to be exact."

With his accent, she'd known it had to be from somewhere south. "You already know I'm from North Dakota, but the town is Oakes. It's minuscule, like less than two-thousand-people."

"Houston was a shock, huh?"

She snorted and then groaned. "Seriously, just call me Wilbur," she said, palming her forehead as Charlotte spelled out her name in the web.

Jax barked a laugh. "Riley, I would never call you that. I sincerely find you adorable, especially when you do that. I meet so many people trying to be anything other than what they are. I'll take authentic every day, all day long."

Another snort popped out. "I wish my ex-boyfriend thought that way." She wished he'd actually cared about her to start with. Finding out he didn't was the reason behind her move a year and a half ago or at least one of the many.

"I'm sorry."

She waved him off. "As much as I hate to say it, it

was probably for the best. He kept me in Oakes, and I needed to leave. It wasn't a good place for me."

"I know the feeling, and," he heaved a sigh, "it can be hard to make that decision because it's all you've ever known, and what if you get to where you're going and it's worse."

Her mouth dropped open. "Exactly. I was terrified. I don't know anyone in Houston, and I felt like an ant most of the time." She chuckled. "I started to make friends at school, but it's hard to build a friendship when you don't have time for them."

Jax laughed. "Yeah, if there's one thing I understand, it's that. I'm on-call, so making plans or keeping dates is impossible." He sat up. "Not to kill the conversation, but there's a gas station."

She faced forward and clapped. "Whew. Good timing." Not only did she need a restroom break, but she needed food. "I'm hungry too."

"Yeah, we'll see what they have, and maybe stock up a little in case we find ourselves on a stretch of road that's lacking. Maybe we'll pick up some gas cans too for the same reason." Jax circled the place, checking for cars, and once he was confident no one was following them, he pulled up to a pump and cut the engine.

He turned to her. "We need to be quick and alert. If anything seems off or weird, let me know."

"Okay."

"Stay right there." He paused as he set his hand on the door handle. "I think it'd be a good idea if people think we're together, so I'm going to hold your hand. I'm just letting you know so you don't think I'm trying to invade your space."

Her planned response was to let him know how appreciative she was that he respected her enough to let her know what he was doing and that she agreed with him that it was a good idea. By the time the sentence reached her lips, however, the letters had rearranged themselves into a sentence so spectacularly embarrassing it made her want to cry. "You can invade my space any time." Oh, heavens. "By the time this trip is over, you'll be surgically removing my foot from my mouth."

The sexy grin he shot her made her glad she was sitting down. "And why would I want to do that when I enjoy it so much?"

No way was she meeting his gaze. "You…you… you… are…"

"I what?" His voice was low and husky.

Her attention jerked to him and she swallowed hard. How did she answer that when her tongue couldn't be trusted? "You're, um, nice."

"Is that so?" Those dark eyes of his held mischief. "Just nice?"

For just a second, she thought that maybe he was

flirting with her, but the situation was stressful, and he was trying to distract her, so she didn't dwell on the situation they were in.

"Yes, you're nice. You knew I'd feel bad, and so you were just playing it off."

Something flashed in his eyes, and she could have sworn he was a little disappointed with her response. That wasn't true though, and she knew it. It was the same as him ordering extra food. He was saving her from embarrassment that was all. And while she knew there was no way he'd be interested in her, she had a bad feeling that by the end of this, her heart would be so broken, she'd never find all the pieces.

8

 $\mathcal{T}$ he stop at the gas station was as quick as they could make it. The selection of maps was abysmal and all would have taken him west. Now, he was kicking himself that he'd left Houston without one. Maybe the next station they stopped at would have a map and a few gas cans. The Power Wagon was turning out to be one thirsty vehicle.

He *had* purchased a burner phone, and was glad Noah suggested it. They were on roads with little traffic and if they happened to break down, having no form of communication sounded like a bad idea. Hopefully, they wouldn't need it at all, and it would remain unopened.

When he swerved off the road, it was his cue that he needed to stop for a bit. "I'm exhausted. I'm going to look for a place to hide and get a little sleep."

"Okay."

Roughly forty-five minutes later, he was pulling into an abandoned gas station with a garage bay. "This should be good for a few hours."

"Would you like to stretch out? It's okay with me if you do."

"No, I better not. I'm just wanting a catnap. With as relentless as they were in Houston, it makes me nervous to stay too long."

"Okay, but if you change your mind, let me know."

Sheesh, she was sweet. "Thank you."

He leaned his head back and closed his eyes, but as tired as he was, he couldn't turn his thoughts off. He'd met Riley less than twenty-four hours ago and he already liked her more than most of the women he had ever met.

She'd asked him why he'd become a doctor, and there was a longer story there than he was comfortable sharing just yet. It'd been a surprise that she'd dropped it and moved on. The few women he'd dated in the past had pressed him, and that'd been a complete turn off.

Another point in her favor was the fact that she hadn't asked about his dad. He'd been bracing for it too. With the way he'd reacted, he probably would have had he been in her shoes. She was perceptive.

High school diploma or not, that wasn't a character trait that most possessed.

Without realizing it, he'd managed to doze off and as the sun peeked over the horizon he woke up and found the closest pit stop to fill up the truck again. When he was a kid, he'd had no idea how much gas it took when he and his dad went camping. Pulling the camper would have made it even worse. How had his dad even afforded it? It wasn't like they were super rich when he was kid. They'd even used paper maps when they traveled.

"Hey, it just occurred to me. Would you check the glove box? There might be a map in there." He should have checked it before they left Houston, but he wasn't exactly thinking clearly at the time.

Riley held the beef stick she was eating between her teeth and opened the glove box. She made a little squeak—the kind that said, I found something—and pulled out the contents, setting them on her lap. Taking the stick from her mouth, she nodded. "Yep, there is." As she opened it, she whined, and her shoulders sagged. "Aw, it's a map but not one we need." Something fell onto the floorboard, and she picked it up, sucking in a sharp breath. "I think your dad left you a letter, Jax."

He jerked his attention to her. "What?"

She held it up. "A letter."

Sure enough, there was Jax's name scrawled out in his dad's handwriting.

Her head tilted and she laid the beef stick on the dash before picking up a small, notebook-type thing. "There's also a small photo album."

First the storage unit, now the letter and photo album? For over two decades, the man was a ghost, and now, all of a sudden there he was bashing Jax over the head with memories he didn't want to relive.

"Are you okay?" she asked.

"I haven't been okay since I found out my dad left me that storage unit. I just don't know what he could possibly say that would change anything." It was an outburst he didn't need to make. Keeping his eyes on the road, he worked to put all the memories in a file and slam the cabinet closed. Once Riley was safe, he'd find a way to muster up the courage to deal with it. "If you don't mind, just put them back."

She placed the items back in the glove box and paused while she kept her hand on them. "My offer still stands, and nothing will change the friendship we have. I promise that."

Words lodged in his throat and the best answer he could give was a nod.

She picked up her beef stick again and took a bite. Of all the things he liked about her, the willingness to put his heart first and her curiosity second was his favorite. Even her soft pushes encouraging him to confide in her felt genuine. Falling for her would be as easy as falling back into a deep pool.

Silence fell between them to a near-stifling degree. He didn't know what to say, and it seemed she didn't either. What was there to say? His heart was broken, and it felt like his dad was dancing on the shards. Part of him wanted to spill the whole pathetic story, and the other didn't want to see the pity in her eyes. He couldn't change what happened. The best he could do at this point was work through it and try to crawl out of the other side with the least amount of damage.

"My ex-boyfriend, Charlie Hoen, was a jerk," Riley said, breaking the awkward silence.

Jax looked at her. He didn't want her to feel like she had to tell a story, so he didn't feel bad. "You don't—"

"Shush."

With a chuckle, he nodded. "Okay."

"Charlie was a jerk. He was sort of the catalyst behind my move."

"Ah." Jax could see that being plenty of motivation for a change in scenery.

"Oakes is home to several grain elevators, and he was a truck driver. I was working at a diner, and he came in before he was supposed to pick up a load. We hit it off and exchanged numbers. The first few months were amazing. When I wasn't working, we were talking. I guess you could say we were joined at the lips instead of the hips." She laughed, gave a small sigh, and shrugged. "With nothing to do but talk, other than when he came to town, we got close fairly quickly. Well, I thought so."

Jax's heart was already beginning to hurt for her. It didn't take a lot of brain power to see where the story was going.

"I was living in a two-bedroom apartment, and I'd offered Charlie the use of the second bedroom when he was in town. One of the reasons he never wanted to stay more than a few hours was because he didn't want to pay for a room when he knew he wasn't going to use it long. I had it, and I wanted more time with him."

She snapped off a bite of her stick and began again. "I thought things were great. We were getting to spend time together; he was talking about having me travel with him. The time was never right though. He always said soon." She grunted. "By soon, he meant never. Turned out he had a woman in almost every city he was in, and he was telling them the same thing he told me."

Jax's mouth dropped open. Dating was hard and dating more than one woman? Count him out. "How many women?"

Twisting in her seat, she huffed. "Including me? More than a dozen."

He jerked his attention to her, his mouth dropping open. With a scoff, he replied, "No way."

She nodded. "Yes, way. We'd been dating a little over seven months when he left his phone in the living room while he was taking a shower. Someone must have been looking out for me because he never did that, and as I was walking by the end table it was on and…a text popped up. Talk about a rabbit hole. We were in his phone as the name of the city we were in."

Jax grimaced. "Sheesh. That's really…gross. I wish I had a better word." Jax shook his head, feeling like he needed to shake the slime off. "I'm so sorry." He glanced at her just long enough to catch her smile.

Her gaze lowered to the seat. "At the time, I was devastated, but then I realized I wasn't as upset as I should be." She cleared her throat. "After that, I moved to Houston and signed up for nursing school. I'd made it through the first semester and signed up for classes in the spring when I got laid off of my job. By the time I landed the one with the import company, I'd run through my entire savings."

"That's…that's awful. I'm so sorry." None of the words seemed strong enough to truly express what he felt.

She sniffed and blinked a few times. "Anyway, on to another topic. Do you like working for Guardian Group?"

Yeah, he'd want to move to a different topic too. "I do. Being on-call gets tiring, but I love it. People will come to us and have nowhere else to go. Noah isn't like most people in the private security business."

She tilted her head. "How so?"

"He includes the people we protect. Many times, they're kept out of the plan, it strips them of their choices, and leads to distrust which is the last thing you want when trying to protect someone."

"That's why he asked you if I wanted help."

Nodding, Jax replied, "Yes, and I was serious when I said you could leave and that it would have killed me to let you." He glanced at her and found her smiling.

"I really didn't want to face him alone, so...I'm—"

"Hold that thought," Jax said as a dark sedan pulled alongside the truck and careened into his lane. He jerked the truck to the left to avoid getting hit. It was broad daylight, but they were on a stretch of road that seemed less traveled.

Sunlight glinted off metal. "Get down!" Swerving to avoid the weapon aimed at his window. He jerked the wheel to the left, trying to push them into the ditch and missed as they slowed their car.

He slammed his foot down on the pedal, and the engine let out a growl that would have made Jax smile, if he hadn't been trying to outrun someone who was trying to kill them. The 440 engine that his dad had rebuilt was just as fast as Jax remembered.

The car caught up, and the truck jolted to the side when the sedan rammed the bumper. They were in the middle of nowhere, and he needed to lose these guys. Nowhere to hide, no way to ask for help. As much as he hated the idea of damaging the truck, he suspected there was really no other option than to use it. That plastic sedan was no match for solid metal.

"Riley, you need to brace yourself and hold on. I'm going to try to lose them. Okay?"

"Okay."

Jax checked the side mirror, waited until the car was next to him and slammed on the brakes. As he did, he cranked the wheel hard to the left, hitting the bumper of the car. It spun out, hit the gravel lining the road and flipped while the truck wobbled hard before it stabilized.

He punched the gas once again, and as soon as the car was out of sight, he looked at Riley. "Are you okay?"

The only answer he got back were tiny little whimpers that broke his heart. He looked at the burner phone on the floorboard. There was no way they could have been traced with it. Even the gas station they'd stopped at had been the only one he'd seen in miles.

"Riley?"

She sniffled and pulled herself up. "I'm okay."

Groaning, he raked his hand through his hair. "I'm so sorry. I should—"

The motion of her hand wiping away tears caught his attention. "Not have volunteered in the first place."

He cut at glance at her. "Yes, I should have, and I need to be more aware," he said, checking the side mirror. "I just don't know how they found us. We're not connected to anything. The radio doesn't even work."

"Yeah, I don't either..." The way she said it sounded a little off, but someone had just tried to run them off the road. He couldn't say he didn't sound off too.

How on earth had they been tracked? He wasn't even sure what road they were on, and out of the blue, a dark sedan just pulled up next to them? If they'd been followed since Houston, there was no way they would have made it as far as they had without some sign that they were there. There wasn't even a car in the parking lot at the last gas station. He knew because he'd circled it to make sure there weren't.

So, how on earth had Galen White's men found them? That was going to eat at him until he had an answer. In the meantime, he needed to make more tracks and drive as far as his body and the gas tank would allow before they stopped again. Obviously, they'd need to be more careful this time too.

Between the jetlag and all the chaos, he was feeling the wear of the day. Even accounting for the small nap, Riley was probably feeling worse. As soon as he was certain they weren't followed, he'd stop. Although, his confidence was markedly lower now after what had just happened.

Still, they'd both need a break to stretch their legs, and he'd just have to hope that he'd slowed them down enough that they could stop, eat, and rest a little. Maybe the next store would carry a map they could use, and hopefully he'd figure out a route that would get them to North Carolina safely.

9

*R*iley was lost as a bug in a snowstorm. Jax had zigzagged and taken so many side roads, someone could tell her she was on the moon, and she'd believe them. Maybe that was a stretch too far, but it sure felt like it.

The sun was winking at them before Jax felt comfortable enough to stop in a tiny little Arkansas town. It was a two-lane road with a diner, a stop sign, and a motel. Two out of the three things they needed most, so it'd been perfect.

Just in case trouble found them, a real meal was the first order of business, especially since the diner had restrooms. With the camping gear, if they had to, they could bolt if trouble found them and stop somewhere else.

Now, as she sat across the table from him, she

wished they'd gotten something to go so they could find a place and let him rest longer. The dark circles around his eyes along with his thickening accent said he was exhausted.

"I think I'll go basic. Eggs, bacon, and some orange juice." He smiled, but his eyes didn't have the sparkle in them they'd had when they first met. He covered his mouth with his hand as he yawned. "You may need to drive a little bit if we're found before I can get a little shut eye."

Oh, no. Drive? Her heart hit her toes. She rolled her lips in and lowered her gaze to the table. "Um…I kind of don't know how to drive."

"What?" He blinked and his voice rose an octave.

She squeezed her eyes shut, grimacing. Images of Charlie laughing at her floated to mind. That had been a hiccup in their relationship early on. He'd made so much fun of her. Almost cruelly so. "I don't know how," she said softly, bracing for the coming barrage of laughter.

Lifting her head a fraction, she found his mouth hanging open like she'd just said she was from Mars. Which, given how unlikely it was that someone her age wouldn't have her driver's license, wasn't unexpected.

Groaning, she hung her head. "I know. I'm such a loser."

A current of air moved and when she looked up,

Jax was seated next to her. His gaze caught hers and held it. "You are not a loser because you don't know how to drive. My best friend never learned how to drive. He was autistic. Super high functioning, wicked smart, and an all-around great guy. He would freeze when things got a little too stressful. He didn't trust himself and he didn't want to be the cause of a car accident." He smiled. "If you want to learn, I'll be happy to teach you. Otherwise, Mrs. Daisy, I'll just keep driving." He winked.

Riley caught her bottom lip between her teeth, working to hold back actual tears. Instead of making her feel worse, he treated her with kindness. Jax had to be the sweetest human being she'd ever met, and the most wonderful man on the planet.

"You've been nicer to me than anyone I've ever met."

His head tilted and his eyebrows knitted together. "That doesn't make sense to me. I've enjoyed your company since the moment we met. You're real and down-to-earth. You saw something wrong, something evil and you took the initiative to try to right a horrible wrong." He swallowed hard and cast his gaze to the table. "And you haven't pressured me into talking about things I'm not ready to talk about. If my opinion matters, that alone makes you amazing in my book."

If? Her little heart squealed with delight. His

opinion was quickly becoming the only one that mattered to her. Not once had he looked at her like she wasn't worth having around. He was a guy girls only dreamed of meeting. "Thank you."

He wrapped his arms around her and kissed the top of her head. "I'm sorry so many people have mistreated you and made you feel like you were less than. I won't let it happen anymore. Even when all of this is over, I'll be happy to fly to Houston and deck anyone who messes with you."

When this was all over? She didn't like the sound of that at all. They were in a horrible predicament, and part of her never wanted it to end just so she could spend more time with him. She hugged him around the waist and melted into him. If she could make time stand still, she would. Being held by him was the best thing ever. He was warm and kind and wonderful and she never wanted him to let go.

Leaning back, Jax caught her gaze and the world fell away. She'd never wanted to kiss anyone or be kissed by anyone so much in her life. What caught her off guard was the feeling that he wanted to kiss her too and in the current hallucination she was having, his lips were even moving closer to hers.

A clearing of the throat broke through the little paradise of a bubble, and Jax returned to his seat. The waiter glanced from Riley to Jax and grinned as he set glasses of water in front of them. Riley's cheeks were so hot they could probably fry eggs. Maybe a few slices of bacon too.

Once he'd taken their orders, Jax set his elbows on the table and put his head in his hands, sighing. "That nap is wearing off. I want a shower, a bed, and nothing but the back of my eyelids for about twelve-hours." He looked at her and chuckled.

"No kidding." She waited a beat and then asked, "Were you serious about teaching me to drive?" It scared her, but it was worth facing her fear if she could help him. He'd done so much for her, and it felt selfish not to try to at least return a fraction of his kindness. Plus, he had a gentleness about him. If anyone was going to be patient with her, he was her best bet.

"Yeah, I was, but like I said, only if you want to."

"I want to." She hugged herself. "My dad tried to teach me, but he was a little gruff on a good day. Not in a mean or abusive way. He was just used to telling people to do something, and they did it. Our personalities were completely opposite, and we clashed more than once. I was stuck in the middle, and my mom was too busy with my siblings' sports and other extracurricular activities, she just didn't have time."

"It was a little like that when I was growing up, so I can relate to that." A small grin lifted the corners of his lips.

"I was the easy kid with little to no maintenance. I got good grades, I had a few friends, and I kind of blended into the background. I guess my mom and dad got too accustomed to that, it made it easy to overlook me."

Jax's hands dropped to table as he leaned forward a little. "That had to be hard."

Shrugging, she replied, "Maybe a little when I was younger, but now that I'm older, I can better understand. I was smack dab in the middle of seven. My mom was always going, always doing. We were a busy family, and when I look back, there are times that my mom would say little things that gave me the impression that she appreciated and loved me for being easy."

"That's a pretty mature way to look at it, and they must have done something right because I think you're great."

For a second, she didn't know what to say. Typically, when she told people how many kids were in her family, they'd be floored. She tilted her head. "Nothing about the fact that I was one of seven?"

"I was one of twelve most of the time. The number changed pretty frequently." His eyes grew stormy, and his gaze lowered to the table. "I don't really like to talk about it."

She stretched her arm across the table and covered his hand with hers. "And you don't have to. Ever. But if you ever decide to, know that it'll never go anywhere else. And if I have to fly to Mississippi and kick some rear end, I will."

His shoulders bounced as he laughed. He lifted his gaze to hers, and his lips were quirked in a half smile that made her glad she was sitting down. Oh, this smile was the best one yet. Sexy and flirty and everything good in between. "I may have to take you up on that offer."

Her heart squealed in delight and shouted *please*. Even her head didn't have an argument about that. If her knight in shining armor needed a queen in shining armor, she'd happily take on that mantle.

Then reality popped its ugly head up and reminded her that they were being chased and it was possible that all these feelings had more to do with her situation. Still, he'd helped her and if he needed her help in the future, he'd have it.

The waiter returned to the table, setting their drinks and plates in front of them. "Enjoy, and if you need anything, just holler."

Riley inhaled the aroma. Either this was the best breakfast joint in the world, or she was just so desperate for good, hot food, that it didn't matter.

"I knew I was hungry. I didn't realize I was ravenous. I think I could tip the plate up to my mouth and rake it in," Jax said, laughing.

"No joke." She lifted her ham a little and looked at his plate. "The bacon looks awesome. I didn't order any because I'm picky, but it looks like it's the perfect combination of crispy and soft."

"I don't mind sharing. That ham looks good. Like it's the kind you slice off a spiral."

They spent the rest of their meal trading items and discussing the vast benefits of a good, hearty breakfast. After they'd finished, Jax paid for their meal, they returned to the truck, and drove all of about a block to the motel. Just seeing it made what energy she had ebb away.

Jax pulled into the parking lot and scanned the area. "I'm not sure I'm comfortable stopping."

"What? Why?"

He tipped his head to the gas station across from them. "Those guys are as big as the ones we've been dealing with, and they're staring pretty hard at us."

Riley took a moment and swept her gaze left to right. "Yeah, it seems so, but this truck is pretty cool. It's not like you see something like it all the time. They could be admiring it." Or she hoped so. The promise of a soft bed appealed to her in ways it never had before. It made her want to cry thinking about stretching out and having it yanked away.

Nodding, he replied, "Maybe, but… just in case, we'll find another hotel."

Just as Riley had refastened her seatbelt, Jax hit the gas pedal, peeling out of the parking lot onto the road. Moments later, a black sedan much like the one that had tried to run them off the road came racing out.

"I don't know how they keep finding us. Noah said there would be a BOLO out on us, but this doesn't make any sense. This town isn't on a typical path to North Carolina." He huffed. "I think our roughing it, just got rougher."

Riley's shoulders sagged. They were being run ragged. It made her wonder if that was the goal. Exhausted people didn't think clearly. It was easier to make mistakes and they couldn't afford that.

Jax glanced at her. "As much as it hurts to say this, I think we need to ditch the truck and find something else to drive. I have no idea how or where we'll find anything, but I can't see any other way at this point."

All she wanted to do was cry. He'd already given up so much for her, and now his dad's pickup? It wasn't fair to ask that of him. "Jax, you can't do that. This was your dad's pickup, and you haven't had even a second to process it yet." She slid her fingers between the chain and her skin and pulled out the flash drive, letting it dangle.

"What are you..." The rest of the sentence trailed off as his gaze landed on it. "What is that?"

"It's basically a hard drive with all of Galen's files on it. I...I'm sorry."

She couldn't express how deeply sorry she was for all the trouble she'd caused him. He could now take the card, drop her off, and she'd stall Galen as long as possible. Jax could keep his truck, get rid of her, and make it to North Carolina much easier. Hopefully, he wouldn't hate her forever, even if she deserved it.

10

*J*ax jerked his attention to her and gaped for a second. All this time she'd had that? Why hadn't she disclosed it? If they had a set of files as evidence, they could have...done nothing because based on what Mia said, the people working for Galen could have wiped it or whatever computer people did.

She'd gone to the police, and they'd acted suspicious. Even knowing she had a sixth sense, with as chaotic as things were, he couldn't really fault her for not telling him she had it. If Galen was worse than Tom Harrison, he was actually glad she'd been cautious.

"Put it back," he said, returning his focus to the road.

"But—"

"I'm not dropping you off, Riley. You had no idea

who I was or who I worked for. That detective gave you a good reason to be suspicious of people. Once you realized how bad Galen was, it was even more important to keep that thing safe. You did the right thing, so put it back."

"You can't ditch this truck." It came out almost like a plea. Not only had she put herself in danger to stop a horrible human being, but she was also willing to sacrifice herself for the stupid pickup.

"Yes, I can. It's just a hunk of metal. There are real people in those files and if we have a chance to rescue them, to put Galen in jail, then I'm doing it. This truck will never be more important than you or the people Galen is hurting."

"Okay."

This time it wasn't just the 440 that saved them, it was the off-road tires and lifted body that came in handy. He'd gotten far enough ahead he'd taken a weird banjo-feeling dirt road, drove down just long enough that he was sure they weren't trespassing, and plunged them into a forest until he was sure they couldn't be seen from the road. Hopefully, he hadn't damaged the truck and he could get back out once they were clear.

When the threat of getting caught passed, he exhaled, cut the engine, and leaned his head back against the headrest. "I know it's not the most ideal place, but maybe we could park here a second, and rest."

She palmed the spot over her heart and nodded. "I'm okay with that. How long do you think we need to stay here?"

Jax lifted his head and shrugged. "Honestly, I have no idea. The last sign I saw said Alleene, but I don't even know if that's where we are. We could be headed back to Texas for all I know."

Riley unbuckled herself and slid across the seat, hugging him around the neck. "It's okay. You're doing your best and it's more than I could have ever asked for." She leaned back and smiled. "Every delay we have is just more time I get to spend with you, and that's a win in my book."

A win? To him, it felt like everything he did was letting her down. "I just want to keep you safe, and it feels like for every step forward, I take ten back."

Cupping his cheek, she held his gaze. "It's not like we have rules or steps. If I was on my own, I'd probably already be dead. Not probably, I would be dead. Or worse. Those men at the airport had me. I had no idea how to get away, and I knew they were going to kill me. As long as I'm with you, I know I'm safe and that's far more than I hoped for when I stole that drive." She kissed his cheek. "I promise, you'll never be anything less than a knight in shining armor to me."

He held her gaze a moment, the warmth of the tiny kiss spreading across his face. If this was a kiss on the cheek, he couldn't imagine what an actual one might do to him. A thought he needed to shut down. She was being kind, and reading more into that than he should, would be a good way to find himself heartbroken by the time they reached North Carolina.

"Knight in shining armor might be stretching it. Klutz with luck maybe." He smiled.

"Nope, not a stretch at all." She dropped her arms and moved back to her side, patting her lap. "Come on. You've hardly had any rest and since you're the only one who can drive, you need it more than I do."

Between the lack of sleep and the waning adrenaline, his mind was growing foggy and his body felt heavy.

"Jax, come on. It'll be okay."

The longer he sat there, the more exhausted he felt. It wasn't safe to continue. He stretched out with his head in her lap and a long exhale poured out. "Yeah, I need a minute."

Her lips curved into a smile. "I told you so." Then she slid her fingers through his hair and it was like she was sprinkling sleeping dust on him. It was relaxing, comforting, and a bunch of other words he was too tired to conjure. The longer she did it, the heavier his eyes became.

Tree-shaped shadows were being cast across his face the next time he opened his eyes. Riley's head was leaning against the window, and she was breathing evenly. Apparently, they'd both been exhausted.

As he went to move, she jerked awake and palmed his chest. "I'm awake."

"But you weren't," he said with a laugh.

She used the back of her free hand back to shield her mouth as she yawned. "I don't even remember falling asleep." She shook her head, blinking. "But I guess I needed it."

"I feel better."

Nodding, she replied, "Me too. It's quiet and peaceful here."

He pushed himself into a sitting position, stretching his arms across his chest. The little nap had done wonders for him. "Okay. I need a restroom and we can't go on without a map. This driving blind is frustrating me."

"I'm with you on both." She looked out the passenger window. "That underbrush is thick enough it'd be easy to step on a snake, and as wonderful of a doctor as I think you are, a snake bite is the last thing we need."

"Agreed," he said and fired up the engine, praying that they weren't stuck.

Getting the truck out of the hiding spot was easy,

thank goodness. Had the tires or the lift been different, they may have ended up walking. When he hit a paved road, he stopped and leaned forward, looking for the sun. When he found it, he said, "That's west, so I'm going the opposite direction. Or at least as close to that as possible."

Despite not having a map, Jax had managed to get them pretty close to Hot Springs where they found a large, busy truck stop just on the outskirts of town. He pulled into the parking lot and went straight to the back of the lot, stopping between two eighteen-wheelers. The next time he saw Tru's wife, Kayleigh, he'd tell her thanks. They'd met in Mexico, and Tru had been shot. While evading men who were trying to kill them, she'd parked at a large truck stop and hidden their vehicle between two semis.

Setting the brake, he dropped his hands to his lap and laid his head back. "I think we need a different vehicle. The pickup is too flashy and rare, and they're looking for it. We need to find something old, but low-key."

"What will we do with the truck?"

Shrugging, he rolled his head and looked at her. "I don't know. Maybe find a place to store it until I can come back for it."

"I don't like it. You've already given up a lot for me. This—"

"I've given up nothing. We both have the same goal. To stop Galen. The only way we are getting to North Carolina is by leaving it. We're a sore thumb and too easy to spot." He rubbed his face with his hands. "Finding something else is the issue. We need something without a computer chip."

Her eyebrows knitted together as her lips pressed into a thin line, like she was trying to decide if she wanted to argue with him or not. Finally, she nodded and pointed. "You mean something like that?"

Jax followed her line of sight and sat up. When he'd pulled into the stop, he hadn't even noticed the rusted little Beetle with the *for-sale* sign in the window. He'd been joking about the klutz with luck, but now he was wondering if he was onto something.

"Let me check it out." He put his hand on the door handle and turned to her. "If something happens, I want you to grab what you can and disappear. Use the burner phone, call Noah, and tell him what's happened. Maybe there's a better chance of rescue now that we're in Arkansas."

She stared at him a moment with a blank expression, blinking.

"Uh, Riley?" When she still didn't respond, he dropped his hand from the door handle and faced her, his concern growing. "What's wrong?"

"I...I would never leave you. Ever. Not for a

second. I told you we're in this together, and I meant it. If something happens, I'll go down with the ship holding your hand. I'd rather never step foot on land again if it meant you weren't with me. So that is simply *not* an option."

In his mind, he added loyalty to her list of growing attributes. Nevertheless, if something did happen, she needed to go. "That's sweet, but—"

Faster than he thought possible, she slid across the seat and kneeled beside him with her fists balled in his shirt, eyes leveled at him. "No. You said you'd die before you let anything happen to me. What makes you think I don't feel the same way about you? You go check out that Beetle. If something happens, I'll be playing *Grand Theft Auto* until you're safely in the truck again. Do you understand?"

He was dumbfounded, and if this were any other time, he'd be tempted to kiss her. She'd been kissable from the very beginning, and the longer they were together, the stronger it grew. A scene played in his mind of him, standing on the edge of a slope, quickly losing his balance as the word falling began lighting up in neon.

Her grip on his shirt loosened and she hugged him around the neck. "I'll never leave you, Jax, never," she said softly and leaned back, smiling as she locked eyes with him. "Together or not at all. Say, *yes ma'am,* and *I'll see you in a few minutes.*"

Chuckling, he nodded. "Yes, ma'am. I'll see you in a few minutes." Without thinking, he took her face in his hands, kissed her forehead, and opened the door. "I'll be back as fast as I can. Hopefully, we can afford the little bugger."

He shut the door, and as he walked away, he rubbed his face with his hands. What was he doing kissing her at all? It hadn't even taken a second thought. He'd just done it like it was a natural thing to do. If he wasn't careful, this mad dash to North Carolina would end with her name stamped on his heart. She was just so easy to…like. It was easy to picture loving her. It made him wonder what it would be like to be loved by her too.

That faint neon sign grew a little brighter. Man, he was in trouble.

11

*H*e'd paid much less than he'd expected for the Beetle, and then made arrangements to store the truck at the garage. After they'd switched vehicles, they made a run to a big box store. While Riley wasn't thrilled with the idea, Jax's suggestion that they change their appearance made sense. Galen had been in the business a while, and if Noah and Mia were right, he had a network of lowlifes spread throughout the country. So, not only had they grabbed new clothes, but hair dye as well.

From Hot Springs, they'd gone east and found a motel shortly before reaching Tennessee. Not only did they need running water to dye their hair, but they also needed good sleep, Jax especially.

She was still floored that he actually thought she'd leave him there at the truck stop if something happened. After everything he'd risked for her? There was no way. He'd almost seemed shocked when she told him that was a non-negotiable with her. They were either leaving together or not at all.

Riley entered the room and smiled. Two beds. That hadn't even crossed her mind. She appreciated that he was a gentleman without being asked. "Thank you."

Unlike the outside of the motel, the inside felt clean. A small television sat on a dresser-slash-entertainment center, and surprisingly, there was even a small fridge. At the back, there was a bathroom counter with a coffee maker to the left and through the slightly ajar door she could make out a toilet and bathtub.

"Which bed would you like? Lady's choice." Jax did that heart-melting half grin.

"That doesn't seem fair. Which one do you want?"

He looked from one to the other. "If it's horizontal, I'm good."

Laughing, she walked to the bed nearest the bathroom, took her glasses off, and held them as she flopped face-first on the bed.

Until that moment, she'd thought she was a little tired but overall, okay. Now, she didn't want to move for a week, maybe two. It'd been days since she was stationary, and the constant going made her feel like she was still moving. "Oh, wow." She took her glasses off and set them on the bed, glad to have them off her face.

Jax set their things down and collapsed onto the bed closest to the door. "Not the best mattress, but it beats the truck." He groaned. "And now I don't want to move."

"I just might cry for joy."

Something between a moan and laugh came from Jax. "You take the bathroom first, okay?" Jax smiled.

Shaking her head, she replied, "No. You've been driving, and I've had a couple of naps. You need as much time to sleep as you can get."

"I know you're just as tired."

"But you need it more. Plus, if Galen's guys catch up to us, you're the only one who can drive." That little detail was beginning to bug her more and more.

"I can see your point, but I think we'll be okay if you want to go first."

She lifted up on her elbows and leveled her eyes at him. "You know that saying about short women? I'm gonna go Tasmanian Devil on you if you keep arguing with me."

He rolled his head and looked at her, giving her a half grin. "You're so cute." He chuckled.

With that smile? He had it wrong. "I'm short and lethal. Go. Now." She pointed to the bathroom. "March, Mister."

"Fine."

Jax got up, grabbed his bag, and trudged to the bathroom.

What felt like a millisecond later, Jax was gently shaking her awake.

"Hey, Riley, it's your turn." He hooked his finger in her hair, pushing it away from her face. Have mercy. To wake up each day and see that smile. He'd picked a fitted t-shirt and jeans. Whew. Did he ever look good... and had he put on cologne? Whatever it was, she liked it. Fresh and citrusy.

Nodding, she grabbed her glasses, put them on, and pushed herself into a sitting position, her gaze lifting to his hair. He'd picked a dramatically different hair color than his natural dark hue. "Whoa." Okay, so maybe blonde wasn't totally his color, but it didn't matter to her. "You...look...um..."

"Pale as a ghost and weird?" He grumbled under his breath.

Her shoulders bounced as she laughed. "I was going to say, different which is good. That was the purpose of dyeing our hair."

"You were going to say horrible because it's horrible." He ran his hand through his wet hair and little pieces stuck up all over. "If the guys see this, they will tease me until I'm in the grave. Mercilessly and without remorse. And honestly, I may join them."

Riley held her stomach and laughed harder than she had in she didn't know how long. "I'm sorry."

"It's okay. I'll see you when you get out."

She narrowed her eyes. "No, you won't because you'll be asleep."

His eyebrows hit his hairline. "You're dyeing your hair. There's no way I'll be able to sleep until I see it."

"You should at least try. Besides, you'll see it whenever you wake up."

"Fine. I'll try, but no guarantees."

With a nod, she hurried to her feet, swept her bag up, and dashed to the bathroom, leaning her back against the door once it was shut. He'd picked a fitted t-shirt and jeans. Whew. Did he ever look good.

He'd been unaware of the hair shears she'd slipped into the mix of stuff they grabbed. As she'd stood there in the aisle, deciding on a color, she'd had a come-to-Riley meeting with herself. Her hair was long, and it was obvious their description had been broadcast. It had to go. Plus, she'd wanted a change when she moved to Houston. At the time, that didn't include her hair, but maybe it'd be good for her.

An hour and a half later, she was face-to-face with the new her. A brunette with shoulder-length hair, and while it was different, it wasn't *as* horrible as she'd been imagining. She'd thought she'd be shocked and maybe a little teary-eyed. Turning one way and then the other, it grew on her. She'd blow-dried it a little, and it wasn't nearly as dark as she thought it was going to be. Hopefully, Jax didn't hate it.

The thought made her pause. Did she care if he liked it or not? Charlie had always given her grief—more like ridicule—when she talked about doing something different. Maybe that was the root of the question. What if Jax did the same thing? He was probably asleep anyway and wouldn't see it until the next day. If he didn't like it, well, then, he'd just have to deal.

Riley pulled the door open, hesitated a breath, and then stepped out to find Jax sitting on the edge of his bed. How was he still awake? She hadn't even managed that. She crossed the room and stood next to his bed, putting her hands on her hips. He'd said he'd stay awake, but as tired as he was, she was expecting him to be zonked out. "Jax, why are you still awake?"

"Because I saw you put the scissors in the cart. You made a hard decision, and I know that sometimes hair can have an effect on a woman and her perception of herself. I didn't know your attachment to it, and I wanted to be here for you if you needed to talk." He shrugged. "Do you like it?"

Where was a fan when she needed it? She'd never met a man so observant and intuitive. Granted the change was huge, but Charlie wouldn't have noticed it.

The difference between the two men was night and day. "It's okay." She slipped her fingers into it, twirling it around her index finger. "It's growing on me. What do you think?"

"I think it looks great." He ran his fingers through the length of it. "The cut fits your personality too. Short and cute." Then he shot her the sexiest half-smile she'd seen so far.

Inwardly, she was giving her knees a pep talk trying to keep them solid enough to stay standing, otherwise, she'd land in his arms. The thought nearly made her rethink the whole pep-talk thing. "Um… thank you."

His gaze dipped to her lips and back up. She'd never been the girl who kissed a guy first, but she'd also never met a man as tempting as Jax. He was beyond kissable the moment she saw him and getting to know him only made him more so.

As if her brain had taken marching orders from her heart, she stepped a fraction closer and pressed her lips to his. Their gazes locked, and what she saw in his eyes was a full-on war.

"I'm sorry," he said. "I—"

Sorry? Oh, she'd messed up royally. She held up her hand stopping him. Maybe she could salvage a tiny bit of her dignity. "It's okay. Totally okay. We're in a weird, forced-together situation." Hadn't Charlie told her more than once she'd be lucky to find anyone who would put up with her like he had.

His eyes grew stormier as he held her gaze, and he slowly nodded. "Right. We need to get some rest."

"Exactly." She worked to keep her tone neutral while her heart whimpered. From this point on, she'd be keeping her lips to herself.

She also knew that she was right about their situation. It wasn't normal. They were being chased, he was exhausted, and she was a nursing school dropout. In comparison to her family, she was an unaccomplished black sheep. While he'd said that didn't matter to him, deep down, she knew it had to. He was a doctor. Why would he ever want to entangle himself with someone like her? There were plenty of fish in his sea, and she wasn't in it.

Maybe once all this was over, she'd get herself together, get her degree, and then worry about a relationship. That seemed to be the best order. Now her ducks just had to cooperate.

She rolled her eyes as a mental picture of the little quackers formed the word *fallen* while she eyed a cliff as clouds floated by spelling out the word *jump*. Stupid ducks. Rude clouds. Both could take a long walk off a short pier.

12

*J*ax checked the rearview mirror, grimaced, and ran his hand down the mustache and beard that'd grown over the last few days. Not only did his hair look awful, but now he was dealing with itchy facial hair. It'd take a monumental amount of fortitude to make it to North Carolina without shaving it.

Unlike him, Riley looked great. The moment she came into view, his pulse hit a level that would have required prescription medication. She was flat-out beautiful to start. The cute little cut, the way it danced just above her delicate shoulders. She'd been a vision in a t-shirt and pajama pants.

Glancing at her, the memory of her kissing him floated to mind. He'd been so torn. He'd loved the feel of her lips, and it'd taken everything in him to not take her in his arms and kiss her until he had his fill.

They were in a weird, high-stress situation. His goal was to get her to North Carolina safely, not take advantage of her. In his mind, that's exactly what he would have been doing and he couldn't do that to her. He knew he'd made the right call when she backed away and apologized. Now, he'd spend the rest of the trip knowing how soft her lips were, yet also knowing he'd never get to feel them again.

From the moment they woke up, there'd been a fizzy tension between them with little to no eye contact, short questions, and the most basic of answers. He just wished he knew how to fix it.

Riley cleared her throat and twisted in her seat. "So, what was it like being in the Navy? Do you still have friends who are enlisted?"

Inwardly, he expressed his eternal gratitude. For the life of him, he couldn't figure out a way to break the silence. "I liked it, but I was glad to get out. As far as friends, not really. I kept to myself. When I said I studied a lot, I meant it. The guys would want to go out, and I didn't."

"Before Galen hired me, I'd made a few friends. After getting the office job, I re-enrolled in nursing school and there went all my time. It's hard to keep friends when you're never able to hang out."

"That had a lot to do with my lack of social life. When my best friend Mike..." He stopped short, swallowing hard.

"Don't tell me until you're ready to tell me," she said softly as she covered his hand with hers and quickly pulled back.

He glanced at her. "What?"

"I told you about my ex-boyfriend, and now you feel like you're obligated to tell me things. I told you that story because I wanted you to have it. You've risked your life for me, and I don't have anything tangible to make it up to you."

His brain stuttered for a second. How could she even think that? "Riley, even if you didn't have those files, *you* alone would be tangible to me. It's hard to talk about Mike because I see the pity in people's eyes. It makes his memory feel cheap and like I'm using him for sympathy when I just..." They were foster kids unworthy to be remembered, or that's how he'd felt growing up.

"Want to celebrate his life? To keep his memory alive?"

That was the best way he'd ever heard it put. Which meant if he was going to tell anyone, it'd be her. "Until I joined Guardian Group, he was the only friend I'd ever had."

"When did you meet him?"

"In the group home just before I turned nine. He got there a few weeks after me. New kid or not, no one messed with him because he was huge. To be honest, I was little scared of him at first. He ended up bunking with me, and I knew how I'd felt when I first got there, so I gave him a candy bar. Come to find out, his grandma had died, and he didn't have any relatives willing to take him. He'd later tell me that the candy bar was the nicest thing anyone had done for him since his grandma died."

She gasped. "That's awful."

"He was autistic, he'd had trouble in school. Doesn't excuse it, but when I look at it now, I can somewhat understand." He shrugged. "Anyway, the next day at school, it was the usual. There were four bigger guys giving me a hard time. They'd corner me in the playground every day, and it was brutal. If they weren't saying horrible things, they were beating the tar out of me."

"You didn't tell anyone?"

He shook his head. "Uh, no. That would have only made it worse. The one rule at that school was *snitches get stitches*." He chuckled. "Next thing I know Mike is putting himself in front of me and telling them if they didn't back off, they'd be dealing with him."

She leaned her head against the seat, smiling. "He was brave."

Nodding, Jax replied, "He was, and that first confrontation landed us in the principal's office. No one would tell who started it, and since Mike and I were from the group home, it was pinned on us, and we got two weeks of detention. After that, we were best friends."

He chuckled to himself. Talk about the day burned into his memory. Going to school had been a nightmare. Jax never knew when those boys were going to pounce. "I helped him with the classes he struggled with, and he roped me into joining the robotics club—the battle type robots—and he took the school to the finals. We stayed in that club until we went to high school, and then we signed up for a mechanics class. It was a new thing the school was doing, and it was cool. Mike was gifted. Like, the guy could look at something and know what was wrong."

"It sounds like he was a great guy and friend. Did he want to be a doctor?"

Sinking down further in his seat, Jax shook his head. "No, about a week away from graduating high school, we were skateboarding and goofing off, talking about college. Mike had an invitation to join a national robotics team. I was still trying to decide what I even wanted to do." He exhaled softly. "In the middle of a trick, he fell to the ground and died. He'd had a massive heart attack." He worked his jaw. "In the moment, I felt like I should have been able to help him. He'd had my back so many times, and the one time he needed me, I let him down. I mean, I know logically that's not true, but…"

"It felt true."

"Yeah, it did…sometimes, still does." Jax smiled. "I wish you could've met him. He'd like you."

Riley pulled his hand from his lap, held it between hers, and he didn't have words for the level of comfort it gave him. "It's okay to feel like that." She rubbed her thumb over the back of his hand. "For what it's worth, he'd be proud of you. His first act was to protect you, and now, you're working for a group who does that all the time."

Huh. He'd never thought about it like that. Whether Mike would be proud of him was debatable. It wasn't like he was protecting anyone. He was just a physician. A regular, plain ole' doctor who didn't do any of the protecting. He patched up the guys who were the real heroes so they could get back to work. In reality, he was the medical equivalent of a waterboy.

"Just because you don't physically go out and protect people doesn't mean you aren't an equal. Those men in your care wouldn't be able to do what they do without you. You give them peace of mind because they know if anything happens, you'll be there for them."

He appreciated the kindness, but it simply wasn't true. Instead of arguing with her though, he replied, "Thank you for that." He pulled his hand free and shifted in his seat, desperately needing the conversation to move away from him. "Tell me about your family."

Riley tilted her head as if deciding what detail to share. "My dad was a truck driver, he's retired now. My mom designs cards and sells them online. Now that we're all grown, she's moved into painting as well. If I only had a tenth of her talent, I'd be set."

Jax looked at her, smiling. "I can appreciate art, but it's not my talent. I'm lucky if my stick people aren't crooked."

Riley laughed. "Same. My oldest brother, Jack is talented like that. Well, anything he wants to do really. Art, science, math, you name it. Sharolyn is a year younger than him. She's part of a research team in Antarctica. Then there's my sister Anita who is a year younger than her, working on her PhD in aeronautical engineering. My sister Yasmin is thirteen months younger than me. She lives in California with her husband who is an up-and-coming documentary film director. My sister, Teresa, who is a little over a year younger than her is a clothing designer who lives in New York. And last but not least, my brother Dylan is a minor league pitcher in South Carolina."

"Wow." That almost made him thankful he'd only had Mike. He didn't really consider the other kids his brothers and sisters.

"I was the odd duck. My siblings were outgoing and popular, and I was shy and goofy. I mean, I could trip over my own feet."

"Oh, I bet it wasn't that bad."

"Yes, it was." She laughed. "I have a scar just below my chin where I cut it from literally doing that. I did it with style too. Skirt over my head, books strewn all over the school hallway, and nearly the entire school as witness because I did it on the way to class after lunch. I was mortified."

He grimaced. "Oh, ouch. That must have been brutal."

A grunted laugh came from her. "Oh, it was. My senior year, the yearbook gave all the seniors a half page feature. They went alphabetical which meant the homecoming queen shared my page. While her entry listed off her accomplishments, mine recounted that fall in middle school."

Jax palmed his chest. "Oh, I feel that right in the heart. I'm so sorry."

"You know, at the time, it was horrible. Now that I look back, I don't care. I am who I am." She took a deep breath and let it out slowly. "I think life is a series of forks in the road, and our job is picking which to take. Sometimes, we pick a side and there are more bumps in the road than we care for. Other times, we pick a side and while the road is smooth, nothing is learned. I think the rougher the road, the more we learn to find joy in the potholes."

Man, did she have a way of making him speechless. Joy in the potholes. He swallowed down the lump in his throat and nodded. "Yeah."

Now that he was thinking about it, Mike's death had overshadowed all the good memories Jax had. All the times Mike had helped him fix his phone, the times he'd helped Mike with English. Playing basketball and skateboarding. Their shared love of comic books.

From the moment he realized his dad had ditched him, he'd taken the trials life had thrown at him as just one more hit. As if his lot in life was to be the universe's punching bag. To be abandoned and lonely.

As much as that felt like the truth, it wasn't. His mom left, and the next two weeks, his dad spent as much time with Jax as possible, even missing work. He'd been dropped off at the babysitters, but he loved being at her house because she made the best cookies ever and watched superhero movies with him. Then there was the foster home. Yeah, at first that was tough, but he wouldn't have met Mike.

Jax's glass was never half full; it was tipped over and the water was ruining the wood floors. Not once had he appreciated the fact that he wasn't thirsty and it didn't matter how much water he had. Maybe it was time to stop wallowing in all the terrible things and appreciate the blessings that wouldn't have happened without them.

13

*J*f Riley wagered a guess, she'd say they'd
gone at least two thousand miles over the
last two days, but that was probably just her body
protesting the amount of time she'd been in the car.
Aside from stopping here and there for short naps and
quick bathroom breaks, they'd been slowly making
their way east.

The sun was high in the sky as she rolled her shoulders, trying to ease the tension in her neck. Her seat
was barely more than a metal frame, and she was sure
her rear end was becoming permanently ground into it.
"Jax, I need a break from this car."

"Uh…" He grimaced.

"We've changed vehicles and our appearances. We
don't have to do anything fancy, I just need a walk, a
stroll, just something that isn't this car."

Jax took a deep breath, letting it out slowly like he was debating how to respond. "How about a compromise? We stop somewhere, get something to eat, and go from there."

While it wasn't exactly what she wanted, it was better than nothing. He *was* trying to keep her safe, and they still had no idea how Galen's men were finding them. "Okay."

Twenty minutes later, Jax turned into the parking lot of a cute diner called Sweetie Pies emblazoned on a sign next to a woman holding a pecan pie.

Riley's mouth watered to the point she discreetly checked herself. "I want a slice of that pie to eat while we're here and then another to go."

Jax's shoulders bounced as he laughed. "I'm with you. Not sure about the pecans, but I could go for a few slices of peach pie."

Instead of taking a spot in front of the restaurant, he drove down the side of the building and parked behind the commercial dumpster.

She touched his arm and grinned. "Peach pie. We could get a slice of each, whatever they have." Maybe if she ate enough her rear end would get a little more padding and she could handle the seats better.

Once they got inside, it felt like they were stepping back in time. Black and white checkered floors with tables and chairs from the 50's. The décor lining the walls consisted of photos, newspaper articles, and photos of famous people who'd wandered in from time to time. To add to the feel, an icebox display case of pies was placed right at the door. The entire place smelled so good, Riley's stomach growled.

A waitress in a cute little red checked uniform with the nametag, Cindy, greeted them and led them to one of the booths lining the front of the restaurant next to the wall of windows. Jax took the side so he could keep an eye on the street.

Riley snagged a menu and held it up just low enough she could watch him. He grew more attractive by the day. With him being one of the most attractive men she'd ever seen in the first place, that put him over the top. Enough that she couldn't picture another man ever attaining. When she added lifesaver to it, he was on a plane all to himself.

She smiled, catching her bottom lip in her teeth. Her heart swelled twice its size as he told her about his best friend. Jax trusted her with something so personal and precious. A gold medal wouldn't come close to how wonderful it felt.

Mike sounded like a great guy and a fantastic friend. There was no way she could see him not being immensely proud of Jax. How he could think otherwise baffled her.

He'd had a choice to get involved, and he'd stepped

in without even a moment of hesitation. He didn't have to rush in and help her escape those two men. He didn't have to stay with her to stop Galen. All he had to do was take the flash drive, drop her off, and zip the rest of the way to North Carolina. Instead, he told her to put it back where she had it.

Every decision he made was voluntary, and he chose to be a hero. The men he worked with were given dangerous assignments. They signed up for that when they agreed to work with Noah. Not Jax. He'd agreed to be a physician, but Jax saw a woman who needed help and didn't even think twice about jumping into the fray.

"Why are you staring at me?" he asked as he kept reading the menu.

Whoops. "Because you're cute." She gave him a cheesy grin.

He kept his head down as he shook it, but she could see a blanket of pink coloring his cheeks. "I look terrible."

Tilting her head, she wondered if he was talking about his appearance or something deeper. "Not to me." Not ever.

He lifted his gaze to hers, giving her a weak smile. "Anything look good?"

Cindy stopped at their table, dropped off glasses of

water, and strolled to a nearby table with her order booklet and pen at the ready.

Riley set her menu down and put her elbow on the table with her head in her hand. "Pancakes."

His eyebrows knitted together. "Pancakes? I thought you wanted pie?"

"Oh, I do. I want both." Maybe the sugar high would help her handle the seat better.

He blinked. "Both? That's…that's a lot of sugar if you put syrup on them."

"I'll add a side of bacon."

Shaking his head, he chuckled as he lowered his gaze back to the menu. "That's not going to make it any better. You're going to be high as a kite."

Yes, yes she was, and she would enjoy it the entire time. "What are you having?"

"Shrimp and grits," he said and laid his menu on the table, pushing it toward the end where the waitress could easily pick it up.

In her mind, a record scratched. Suddenly, nothing sounded good. "What?"

He looked at her. "Shrimp and grits. It's delicious."

Her entire body had a negative reaction, like she'd been the victim of a verbal assault. "That's not how you pronounce *gross*."

His head fell back as he laughed the deepest,

throatiest laugh she'd heard so far. "It's really good. You need to at least try it before you say it's gross."

Nope. "You've not only defiled the grits, but the shrimp as well. Neptune is plotting the demise of the person who invented that awful concoction." Seriously, just ew.

Another bark of laughter, only this time, it seemed like whatever was weighing on him was gone. The smile he shot in her direction made her tingle from head to toe. His smiles were the best ever.

Holding his stomach, he replied, "Trust me. You need to try it. It might just surprise you."

"Yeah, I'm thinking no."

Before he could respond, the waitress returned and took their orders.

He leaned forward on the table a little. "Thank you. For the tease about the food."

"I could tell there was a lot on your mind." Plus, it genuinely sounded awful. Oh, she'd try it, but the verdict was already in and it was ick.

"Yeah, I do and…"

"You don't know how to assemble the alphabet in a logical order to convey it properly."

He chuckled. "That's a great way to put it."

Shrugging, she replied, "That's how I felt when Charlie left." She rolled her eyes. "There was a moment where I wondered what I'd done wrong. It didn't last very long because, well, he had a woman in every city. I wasn't even in love with him. He was just…there."

"I was dating someone before I accepted Noah's offer to join Guardian Group. I'd thought our relationship was serious, so the moment he approached me, I called and discussed it with her. His hiring process is long, detailed, and methodical. Two months later, I accept the job offer, sign the paperwork, and I thought we were going to dinner to celebrate."

Riley's heart slowly made its way to her stomach.

"Instead of a celebration, she tells me she's accepted a job in Finland with an engineering firm. I don't know what she expected, but I'd already given my word to Noah. I couldn't break it."

"That had to cut deep."

Nodding, he replied, "It did. All she needed to do was tell me she wanted out of the relationship, and I would have understood." He shrugged. "There was no argument or fight. It was just over."

That made no sense to Riley. How could any woman let him go? Successful, principled, and heroic wrapped in the most attractive package she'd ever seen. "I'm sorry."

"Eh, it's like you said. I should have been more upset or tried to convince her to stay. I think we'd both checked out of the relationship months before. It was comfortable."

Cindy returned with their food and Riley eyed Jax's plate with suspicion. Plopped on top of the white grits were six shrimp with their heads on, and they were staring into her soul, condemning her for allowing their demise.

"They're looking at me."

Jax's entire body shook as he chuckled, shaking his head. "No, they're not."

Did he not see the beady little eyes? She'd been willing to give it a try, but now? No way. "I will stick with my pancakes."

"You aren't even willing to try them?"

"I can't eat anything if it's staring at me," she said as she slathered butter on her pancakes before dousing them in maple syrup.

With a shrug, he picked up his fork. "Okay, but you're totally missing out."

On being haunted by shrimp for the rest of her life? She grabbed her fork and cut off a hunk of her pancakes, stuffing them in her mouth. Heaven in her mouth. The perfect texture, light and airy. She moaned and wilted as the flavor exploded in her mouth. "Oh... if the pies are as good as these pancakes...they'll be fantastic." And she'd be ordering one slice of each.

He scooped up a large bite of grits and a hunk of shrimp, looking as pleased with his as she was with hers. "It's better than I thought it would be."

"I'll take your word for it." She smiled. "You can try mine if you like. I think they're best I've ever had."

His eyes sparkled with mischief. "I would but I can't. I only do trades."

She eyed his plate and pointed her fork at his plate. "I think one of them just winked at me."

Rolling his eyes, he grunted a laugh. "You are too funny."

They sat in comfortable silence, eating and just as she'd decided how many slices of pie she'd be ordering, his eyes widened. "We have to go right now."

"What?" She hastily put her glasses back on, twisted in the seat, and her mouth dropped open. "That's not fair. I didn't even get to try to the pie."

They scrambled out of their seats, nearly running to the back of the restaurant, and stopped as they reached Cindy. "Is there a back door we could use?" he asked, looking over his shoulder.

The waitress followed their line of sight, and four large men exited a black SUV. She nodded. "Yeah, go through the kitchen, take a left." She smiled. "I'll slow'em down for ya. Can't have lovebirds being caged."

"Thank you!" Riley would ignore the last part.

They rushed through the restaurant, checked to make sure they were in the clear, and darted for the car. As soon as they were inside, he started the engine, grabbed the shotgun he'd left at arm's reach, and pulled the car forward until there was a clear line of sight.

"What are you doing?" asked Riley.

"Shooting their tires out. They've got one spare. I shoot out two or three and they're stranded for a while. Get down, okay? Just in case we take return fire."

Nodding, she stuffed herself in the floorboard of the car and stuck her fingers in her ears. She'd been around enough shotguns to know they were loud.

He rolled down the window, aimed, and got two shots off before the men flew out of the diner. She set her glasses next to her on the floorboard as gunfire erupted and buried her face in her knees. Even with her fingers in her ears, she could hear the pops going off. Silently she prayed that they'd get out of this alive and figure out how Galen's men kept finding them.

14

"*R*iley, are you okay?" Jax asked as he sped away from the diner. When she didn't respond, he touched her right hand. "Hey. It's over, and the only way they're following us is on foot."

Slowly, she peeled her face from her knees and took her fingers from her ears. She took a few deep breaths and nodded. "Yeah, I'm okay, but that was a little scary."

"No argument from me." He paused a beat. "We need to figure out how they're finding us. Either they're psychic or we've missed something."

She shrugged. "I've looked at the flash drive. There's nothing on it, and I never connected it to the internet once I took it."

Jax kept his eyes on the road, his eyebrows knitting

together. It made zero sense. They'd done everything humanly possible to stay off the radar, and they'd been tracked to a tiny Tennessee town way off the beaten path. Yeah, he'd slowed them down, but there was more than one group of men hunting them.

Riley picked up her glasses, took her seat, and set them on the dash, hugging herself. "I don't know what to do." Her voice wavered.

Stealing a glance at her, his heart broke. Not only was she visibly shaking, but mentally as well. He scanned the road ahead and saw a spot he thought they could hide for a moment. When he reached it, he cut the engine and turned to her.

"Hey—"

She lunged for him, wrapped her arms around his neck, and sobbed. Instead of giving her useless platitudes, he curled his arms around her and held her. They'd just been in a firefight, she was absolutely traumatized, and all his thoughts were centered on how great it felt to have her in his arms.

He was a certified Neanderthal.

They'd talked about their past relationships, and he'd called his last one serious when all it took was a little digging to know that wasn't even a remote possibility. His heart had been on lockdown for years, and it hadn't even phased him to see her go.

Riley, on the other hand, was the most dangerous

woman he'd ever met when it came to his heart. She was different, raw and real. Something wholly more intoxicating than her beauty. He'd liked her the moment he turned around in the airport and that feeling was quickly changing letters into something much more profound.

As the minutes ticked by, she slowly stopped trembling, and several heartbeats later, she leaned back, keeping her gaze down. "I'm such a wimp."

He tipped her chin up with his finger. As her gaze met his, his heart hit the ground seeing the shame in them. "No, you aren't. That was a lot of gunfire and you're not used to it. That's a good thing, and I don't ever want you to get accustomed to it."

"I know, but I've been the dumb, broken damsel already. Once was enough. I need to toughen up and get myself together."

Shaking his head, he wiped her tears away with his fingers and replied, "Absolutely not. You're not dumb or broken or anything else. You are all sorts of wonderful." And soft and warm and the only woman he'd ever met who fit so perfectly in his arms that he wondered if she'd been tailor-made for him. "I like you just the way you are, inside and out."

Riley held his gaze until the air was charged enough his hair stood on end and those pen-lighted, exquisite, soft lips were mere inches away. He wanted to kiss her so badly it hurt, but he couldn't. Not after being in a gun fight. She was vulnerable, and he wasn't going to be the weasel of a guy who took advantage of the situation. Before he could lose the battle between his head and his heart, he swallowed hard and pulled his gaze from hers.

Her gaze dipped to his shirt, and she grimaced. "I've made a mess of your shirt."

Shrugging, he smiled. "It's okay. It clashed with my hair." Plus, as far as messes went, he had stories that would make her nauseous.

A smile lifted her lips and she looked at him through a fringe of lashes, sending his pulse into a staccato beat. "Thank you."

He held in a grunt, thinking she probably wouldn't say that if she could read his thoughts. "Anytime."

Most likely, she was going into witness protection as soon as they got to the Guardian Group, but he couldn't stop wondering if there was maybe something between them. Yeah, the situation was a factor, but he knew himself well enough to know that his feelings were real. He was falling for her and no matter how hard he tried to reason it away, he couldn't.

He also knew that whatever chances there might be wouldn't happen unless he got her to North Carolina safely. "Let's get back on the road. See if we can put some miles between us and them."

Nodding, she returned to her seat and buckled her seatbelt.

He fired up the engine and pulled onto the street, focusing on what they might have that would allow Galen and his men to continually find them. That shootout had to have attracted some attention from whatever law enforcement was in the area. Although, that wasn't his biggest worry since the men who'd shot *at* them were also wanting to roll under the radar.

Late in the afternoon, there were still no signs of anyone following them which almost made him paranoid. They'd been so doggedly determined it was like he was in a constant state of alert. With the Beetle nearly empty, he pulled into the next available gas station and parked in front of one of the pumps. He pushed the door open, stepped out, and stretched his arms above his head, and worked his legs. All the sitting was getting to him.

Riley followed him, and set her hands on her hips, leaning back like she was trying to stretch her spine. "Oh, my goodness. Those seats."

"Yeah, they're not great," he said, groaning as he looked at the pump. "I keep forgetting I can't use my card."

"I can run in and pay." She nodded to the store. "I mean, I can practically touch it from where I'm standing."

While he didn't like the idea of her going in alone, he also didn't want to leave the car. He pulled a bill out of his wallet and handed it to her. A moment later, she was giving him the thumbs up, and by the time she returned, he was filling up the car.

She stopped at the passenger door. "Uh, something's leaking under the car."

Great. Just what they needed. "What?"

He got on his knees, looked under it, and sure enough, there was a leak. He tapped the puddle with his fingertip and brought it to his nose. "We're leaking oil from somewhere in the cooling tower. It's not an easy fix." He watched it a little longer, counting between drips. At least it was slow. That gave them a little more time before the engine overheated.

"What are we going to do?"

"There's nothing we really can do. It's a complete engine disassembly to get to that part."

Tilting her head, her eyebrows knitted together. "How do you even know that?"

"First car. It was all I could afford, and I think by the time I had to sell it, I'd replaced everything on it. Great car, but it was a money pit because of the previous owner cutting corners. It was rock solid when I said goodbye to it."

A smile slowly lifted her lips. "Well, aren't you full of surprises."

His head fell back as he laughed. "If you say so." The pump clicked and he hung it back up. "Let's hurry with the bathroom break and get back on the road."

They'd gone maybe a mile and he looked at Riley. "Would you get that burner phone out?"

"Sure. Are you going to call Noah?"

"Yeah, with the oil leak, there's only so far we can go before it quits on us. The leak is slow, but I really don't think we'll make it all the way to headquarters."

Once it was working, he had Riley text Noah. A second later, the phone rang, and she put it on speaker. Jax kept his eyes on the road and said, "I don't know how they're doing it, but they keep finding us."

"Mia and Ryder have been fighting cyber-attacks since you left Houston." Papers rustled in the background. "So keep it short."

Riley piped up. "Uh, I have a confession to make."

Jax touched her hand and glanced at her, shaking his head as he mouthed the word *don't*.

Her eyebrows knitted together, and she stared at him.

Trust me.

Everything stopped on Noah's end. "Okay."

"The car has a leak," she answered.

There was a long pause, and Jax was pretty sure Noah understood that wasn't what she was going to confess. "All right. Is it drivable?"

"Yeah, but with the oil leak, I'm not exactly sure how far we'll get," Jax said. "I'll text you when it dies and go from there."

"Code it," Noah replied, and the line went dead.

As Riley set the phone down, she asked, "Why didn't you want me telling him about the drive?"

"You can tell him when we get there. The longer we're on the phone with him, the longer Galen's hackers have to figure out where we are." They'd probably do that without their help, but he sure wasn't going to make it easy.

"Did 'code it' mean to be vague, so we don't give ourselves away?"

He smiled. "Yeah, that's exactly what he meant."

"Oh. Well. Not sure I would have been quick enough to think of that." She shook her head and laughed. "This is why I avoid breaking the law. I think I could look at a pack of gum funny and break out in handcuffs, and my aversion to prison is strong."

For some reason, that struck him funnier than anything had in a long while. "I agree. A life of crime is not for me. I'll stick with bullet wounds and upset stomachs."

Rubbing his knuckles along his jaw, he tossed around ideas on ways to keep them safe once the car died. They were in Tennessee, and straddling the border between it and North Carolina, was the Great

Smoky Mountains. He knew because he and his dad spent almost a year planning a trip there.

Just the thought seemed to rip the air from his lungs. It was hard enough packing the camping equipment in the truck. At the time, he'd prayed they wouldn't need it because of the memories it'd conjure. He also knew that park was the best chance they had if they could make it that far.

"I think I have an idea on how to lose those men. It'll mean roughing it, but it could give us an advantage if they do. Would you be up for a little camping?" It hurt him to even think it, but if it kept them safe until Noah could reach them, he'd just have to deal.

"If it'll keep those creeps from catching us again, I'm up for just about anything."

"Okay. Grab the map. We'll figure out where we are and find the fastest route to The Great Smoky Mountains National Park—"

"Wait. Where?" she asked.

"Uh, the Great Smoky Mountains. Why?"

She opened the glove box and pulled out the contents. "I hope you aren't mad. When we were switching cars, I had a feeling we needed to bring this stuff too." She held up a brochure. "This map is of that park."

Sucking in a sharp breath, now he was even more baffled. Why would his dad have kept this stuff? Why hadn't his dad called him? Obviously, the man knew where he was, and yet, he'd not even tried. Although, if he had, Jax probably wouldn't have had anything to do with him. The only reason he was digging out of his childhood quagmire was because of Riley.

In his head, he counted to ten and then took a deep breath, shoving that emotional rabbit hole away. "That's great."

In typical form, she held his gaze and nodded. "Okay."

He grabbed the phone and texted Noah: It's smoky, but if we have to we'll put the fire out. Hopefully, Noah would be waiting for them when they arrived, if something happened and he couldn't, then there was a summit with a fire tower where they could be picked up. He powered down the phone and handed it back to Riley. "Okay, Noah knows. If he can't meet us at the entrance, we'll have to hike to the fire tower."

"Sounds like we've got a plan." She smiled.

If he kept it together, they did. Every time he turned around, he felt like he was being smacked in the face with his dad leaving him. That bridge he thought he'd burned years ago was rising from the flames like a phoenix. He understood it was trauma rearing its ugly head, but he honestly thought he'd made peace with that part of his life.

Maybe it'd give him the chance to find closure. He

could stand in that park, face the monster under his bed, and finally be free. It was a pothole, and at the fork, and if he had to use every ounce of energy he had, he was going to choose to set down the past once and for all.

15

*C*amping wasn't Riley's idea of an awesome time. To be fair, though, she'd never been camping so she really didn't know what to expect. She'd be with Jax, and even with the danger, she felt a little excited to try it.

"It's a good thing the park isn't very far now," Jax said with his attention divided between the road and instrument panel. He'd been doing that since speaking to Noah.

Instead of backroads, he'd taken the shortest route possible to the park. The closer they got, the more likely they were to either reach it or get close enough to walk. Since the gun fight, there'd been no more surprise chases. It made her itchy because there was no way Galen had given up.

A nagging voice in the back of her mind made her

wonder if they'd fallen into a trap. The bad guys had intercepted the text and knew where they were going and were laying in wait for them. Finally, the feeling got so strong that she couldn't keep it to herself any longer.

"Do you get the feeling that they've backed off, so we'll go to the park?"

He shrugged. "Honestly, I don't know. I can't decipher between feeling that might be true, and paranoia."

Well, at least she wasn't alone. "It feels strange, though, right?"

"It does. If we see anything, we'll figure something else out. Although, the engine might not give us a choice. Who knows. Maybe the closer we get to the park, the less they'll be able to track us."

"I hope so." She just felt so defeated and useless. She took her glasses off, set them on the dash, and rubbed the bridge of her nose with her fingers. Leaning her head against the seat, she let her vision cloud over as the scenery zipped past her.

Useless. It was almost like she could hear Charlie whispering in her ear. He'd used that word so much it'd become synonymous with her name. She'd thought she'd dealt with that a few months after they broke up, but over the last few days, his voice had rung loud and clear in her head.

That gun fight had scared her witless. She'd tried to shake it off as soon as Jax told her it was over, but she couldn't, and it made her feel stupid.

He'd pulled over, and she'd lunged for him. His arms had circled around her as she broke down. He didn't offer any words, just his arms around her, giving her more comfort than she could properly express.

She'd slowly calmed down, and she had no idea how long she'd been in his arms. All she knew was that every inch of her skin was on fire and she could picture being held in his arms for an eternity and it wouldn't be enough.

They way he'd held her gaze as his eyes grew stormy. She thought for sure he was going to kiss her again. When he didn't, she'd tried to psych herself up to take charge by reasoning that she was a modern woman who could kiss him. Then she'd clucked like the chicken she was and took her seat. If the chance presented itself again, well, she was going to…most likely chicken out again but it'd take longer.

What felt like a blink later, she was being gently shaken awake. "What?"

"We're here."

She shook her head to clear it. "I see smoke."

"Yeah, the car started overheating just as we got to the park entrance." He glanced at her. "Do you feel better?"

Oh, she was a terrible travel companion. "Yes, but I feel bad that I keep going to sleep on you. How long was I out?"

"Uh, about four hours or so."

It sure didn't feel that long, but with the sun inches away from midafternoon, it backed him up. "I guess I didn't realize how tired I was." She scanned the area. "I guess something happened and Noah couldn't meet us."

"Yeah, I guess so." He sighed. "At least there was a campsite open not too far from the entrance." He smiled. "Officially, we're staying at a campsite not too far from the entrance. Unofficially, I'm hoping to limp to a campsite closer to the fire tower. It's going to take several days to get there, but because it's on a lookout, it should be easy for Noah to pick us up there."

It was pretty with all the lush, green vegetation. They'd entered through an entrance that most people didn't use, and there were still plenty of people milling about. That also meant that there was a chance someone could be waiting to pounce any minute.

"There sure are a lot of people," she said.

She'd hoped Noah was meeting them deeper in the park, but it was silly to have even thought that. If he was meeting them, he would have been front and center. She just hoped he'd actually gotten the text and would be waiting at the fire tower for them.

Nodding, Jax replied, "It's a popular park. There are several campsites, plenty of trails from beginner to experienced, and horse trails. There's even a Back-country for expert campers, but we'll try to avoid that. You really need to know what you're doing when you go out there because there are a lot of wildlife like bears and coyotes."

For a woman who'd never been camping, that didn't sound fun at all. Days of walking? And now bears and coyotes? It was more like a nightmare. At least they'd have a tent, and hopefully, it'd provide enough protection to keep creepy crawlies and animals out.

"I've been watching, but I haven't seen any vehicles that stick out or people overly interested in us, like they were in that one small town."

Her weird vibe meter was pinging with nothing to back it up. "They could have wised up and changed tactics though."

"That's true, and if it weren't for the oil leak, I'd be tempted to ditch the park and just drive the rest of the way." He patted the dash as the car hobbled into the Ramsey Cascades parking area. By the time Jax put in park and cut the engine, there was no way that car was going anywhere else unless it was by tow truck.

Jax leaned his head against the headrest and took a deep breath, groaning as he let it out slowly. "I honestly don't want to move, but I think my body will revolt if I don't get out of this car."

Boy, did she understand that. "This little car is cool, but these seats are..."

"Horrible? Uncomfortable? Evil? I'd rather walk a thousand miles over hot coals than sit another minute in one?"

She belly-laughed. "You're not wrong."

In unison, they opened their doors and stepped out. Her lower back and rear end were done with the Bug. She stretched her arms over her head and groaned as she sucked in a big gulp of air. Fresh and cool, like her lungs were getting a spring cleaning. "Oh, it feels so good to be standing still."

"Yeah, agreed." He turned in place, a smile quirking on his lips. "My dad and I planned to vacation here. It was going to be my birthday present when I turned nine. We were going to stay two whole weeks and fish, hike, and a bunch of other cool stuff. Well, cool when you're a kid." As his gaze reached hers again, his lips were turned down. Sorrow ebbed from him.

Her heart broke. She walked around the Beetle and hugged him around the waist, squeezing him. He stood rigid a heartbeat before wrapping his arms around her as he lifted her off her feet, burying his face in her neck. This place was raking him over the coals, and he'd sacrificed himself for her. Well, he'd been doing that since he met her, but this felt different, like the place was a whirlpool sucking him in and there was no way to get out.

When he finally leaned back, she didn't have any idea how long they'd stayed like that, only that her toes tingled. Sadness still clung to him, but it seemed to lessen somewhat. "Are you okay?" she asked.

His Adam's apple bobbed. "Truthfully? I don't know." His lips lifted in a weak smile as their eyes locked. "Thank you."

She palmed the side of his face. "I'm not sure if I've said this before, but you're pretty wonderful." She ran her fingers through his hair, pressed her lips to his cheek, and smiled. "The world would be a better place if there were more men like you in it."

"I could say the same about you."

Shaking her head, she grinned. "Nope. You win this one."

As she held his gaze, the world fell away. How many times had she wished for a man like him? He'd be so easy to love. She could picture a lifetime of holding his hand and watching sunsets until they were old and grey.

He hugged her tight once more, setting his cheek against hers, and took a deep breath. She wasn't sure why, but it felt like more than a hug this time. Almost like an unspoken language between her heart and his.

He set her down and shot her a smile that was so gorgeous it should be considered criminal. "We should probably get moving if we're going to set up camp before it gets dark. Maybe we can do a little fishing and have a decent dinner."

"You'll have to teach me to fish."

Leaning in, he softly tapped her nose. "It's a date." He winked.

Whoa. Why did the wink always get her? She spun on her heels, palmed the spot over her heart, and worked to not wobble on her rubbery knees as she returned to the passenger side of the car.

There were about to dive into this park, alone. Just the two of them. Together. Hours on end with no gear shift or seatbelts to keep her in her lane. All she could think was that by the time they reached that fire tower, her heart would belong to him and a plan for the future. Either that or she'd be in so many pieces she wouldn't need witness protection to hide from Galen.

Oh, she was in so, so much trouble.

16

They'd taken a chance when they spotted a trodden path and followed it to the bank of a creek. It'd actually been perfect as there was already a ring of fire retaining rocks and a few downed logs to use as seats.

"This looks like a great spot," Jax said. His mind and body were teetering on the edge of non-functional. "If we go any further, we'll risk setting up camp in the dark."

Riley stopped and looked up at him. "That and you're exhausted."

With a chuckle, he nodded. "Eh, if I had to, I could go a few more hours." Taking the pack off and groaning in relief with the reduction in weight he carried. "On second thought, that's not true."

He'd carefully packed the gear so that the more common stuff was easier to access while distributing the equipment as evenly as he could without it overtaxing Riley. Since she'd never been camping, she had no idea how tedious and hard it could be carrying camping gear.

On the trail, they met plenty of people. With it being May, it was a great time to be at the park, and should any of Galen's people want to hijack them, they'd have to be careful. Although, the farther they traveled into the park, the less people there would be and that's what worried him.

Stretching his back, he rolled his neck and shoulders trying to loosen them. He pulled out the tent, and a wave of his dad's cologne washed over him. It was like he was eight again. Movies played in his mind of them putting this tent up. Even as a kid, he'd grown proficient at building it and breaking it down without any help. His dad had even planned on buying a bigger tent before they took their trip.

By the time it was set up with the sleeping bags in it, his heart was shredded. Every memory was hitting him in the gut, and the more he tried to hate the man, the more he failed. Trying to reconcile the man he knew, with the man who left him and never returned, was turning into a heated battle between head and heart.

He grabbed the fishing gear and parked himself closer to the bank. The tacklebox was the same one he and his dad had used at least a million times. The dirt filled creases of the duct tape wrapped around the handle after it broke hadn't even been changed.

"This is incredible," she said and scanned the area. "We're running from bad guys, but it's hard not to enjoy the beauty of the place." She sat beside him, drawing her knees to her chest and wrapping her arms around them. "Think we'll catch any fish?"

He chuckled. "I hope so. It's been a while since I've been fishing."

Shrugging, she said, "I've never been fishing."

"No better time to learn," he said, returning his attention to the tacklebox and opening it. He picked up his dad's favorite lure and ran his fingers over it. It was ugly as all get out, but it worked. Although, much like the truck and camper, it'd had a little bit of sprucing too.

All the pep talks in the world couldn't have prepared him for the wave of emotions he was experiencing. He knew he had the choice to look at things from a different perspective, but knee-deep in the middle of this mental cheese grater it was hard to focus on the positive.

He'd stepped out of the car, and it was like every memory he had of him and his dad planning their trip played in color. Where they'd go, what they'd do, and all the plans to maximize their time there.

Then Riley came to his rescue. Man, that hug. It'd been so much more than that. Her warmth, her comfort. She was a balm to his soul. He'd held her until his arms ached. When she leaned back, she'd set her hand against his face, kiss his cheek, and it'd taken everything in him not to kiss her.

The more practical side of his brain had caught up, and he knew they'd need to set up camp before it got dark. Had they arrived even a second earlier, he wasn't sure he could have resisted the temptation.

Riley bumped him with her shoulder. "Open ears, and a shut mouth if you need it."

Oh, he needed it, he just wasn't sure he should. All he seemed to do was whine about his past. What if she got tired of it and decided he wasn't worth sticking around for. He certainly wouldn't blame her.

"Jax, it's okay." When he didn't respond, she shifted and leaned across him, tipping his chin up until their eyes met. "Your dad left you when you were nine years old. Finding out he had that storage unit rocked your world and all your beliefs about him were put into question." She smiled and dropped her hand. "It's okay to be angry with him and love the memory of him at the same time."

He was hobbling down memory lane with broken ankles and no crutches. He could only handle so much before he flopped down and caught his breath.

"This was our thing. I mean, we went hunting too, but fishing was where we would sit and talk. He'd tell me about my grandpa and grandma. I'd tell him what I wanted to be when I grew up." He looked at her. "Astronaut or race car driver."

Her lips curved up, and she wrinkled her nose. "I can picture Halloween now. I bet you were adorable."

He grunted a laugh. "Thank you." Shaking his head, he cleared the thoughts. "We're losing daylight. If we want to eat something besides protein bars, we need to hustle."

"I'd prefer fish." She grinned.

Until now, he'd avoided anything and everything to do with fishing or outdoors. It'd been part of his identity that tied him to his dad, and he'd wanted no part of it. Yet falling back into it was easy too. As a kid, it was his favorite thing beyond just talking to his dad. He loved the sport of it.

They dug around and gathered up a few worms, dumping them in one of the compartments of the tacklebox. For someone who'd never fished before, he'd figured he'd stay away from fly fishing until she got a little experience under her belt.

Unfortunately, she wasn't exactly a natural at fishing, but she certainly had the drive and the spirit to learn. Of course, she'd gotten frustrated with herself which only made it worse. Well, funny too. It seemed she had a penchant for getting her hook caught in everything but a fish.

He enjoyed this, the easy pace, the ability to quietly reflect and regroup, and he was done avoiding it. Yeah, there'd be memories, but he could make new ones. It wasn't just being with his dad that made him enjoy camping and the outdoors. As an adult, he could see striking out on a trail and losing himself in the quiet.

Once he'd caught enough fish, he cleaned them while she gathered wood for the fire. As the saying went, it was like riding a bicycle. He'd thought there'd be a little challenge, but the skills he'd learned as a kid easily returned. As the fish cooked, they'd kept the conversation light and mostly focused on how fantastic dinner smelled and they'd tasted even better.

"Jax?"

He blinked and shook his head. "Uh, yeah?" He hadn't even realized he was holding the letter his dad wrote, flicking one of the corners.

She'd taken a seat on the ground facing him without it even registering. "I have no money to pay you for your thoughts, but I'll give you an IOU if you want to talk."

Did he? No? Yes? It felt like he'd been tossed into the ocean with weights tied to his ankles and he was desperately trying to break the surface. He was so tired of it. Would the letter even give him answers? Did he want to know what they might be? "I can't decide if I want to read it or burn it."

She nodded.

"I'm drowning and I feel pathetic. I'm thirty-six years old and still afraid…" He squeezed his eyes shut as he exhaled and shook his head. "I…"

"You're afraid if you open it, it'll break you. That it'll contain all your worst fears. In the back of your mind, you've worried that you were the reason your dad left you." She clamped her hands over her mouth. "I didn't mean to say that out loud. I'm so sorry."

Hammer meet nail. She'd taken his alphabet soup and arranged it into words that said everything he was thinking and was unable to speak. "Don't be. That's exactly how I feel. I was almost nine when Mom left, and looking back, I was angry with him because I thought it was his fault. For years after, I figured that's why he'd taken off. I'd been so mad and I'd taken it out on him."

Scooting closer, she cupped his cheek and held his gaze. Instead of pity, he saw an understanding that he'd never felt before. "I don't have to read that letter to know that had nothing to do with it. You were a kid. Your dad understood that."

"Maybe," he said, stretching his legs out, crossing them at the ankles.

Dropping her hand, she replied, "I'm certain of it."

He groaned. "I feel so stupid. I'm a grown man and it's like I'm stuck in time, watching him drive off, not realizing it'd be the last time I'd see him."

Without a word, Riley circled her arms around his neck. "I've got you, Jax," she whispered. "I've got you."

"I'm supposed to be taking care of you," he said, wrapping his arms around her and crushing her to him as he pulled her across his lap.

A heartbeat ticked by and the next time she spoke her voice. "We're supposed to take care of each other."

If this kept up, he'd be so addicted to her by the time this was over, he'd go through withdrawals. He buried his face in her neck, taking a deep breath, and then slowly breathed her in. Every time he held her, peace settled over him. It felt right to have her in his arms, and each time he held her the colder he'd feel when he let her go.

The word *falling* was in full color and *fallen* was quickly taking its place as his balance continued to deteriorate. She was soft and warm and all the things he'd wanted in a woman. When he pictured them parting ways, it felt like a piece of him would be ripped away.

This. The fire, the quiet, and her. This was his definition of paradise on earth. He lifted his head, scanning the area, and he could see the sunset through a hole in the foliage. "Riley, you need to see this."

As she followed the direction of his finger, she gasped. "It's beautiful."

The sunset was amazing, but on his list of beautiful things, it was coming in second place to her. "Yeah, it is."

She rested her head against his chest and sighed. "Houston was so busy and chaotic. I might have to make this place a yearly visit to regroup and refresh." She yawned, snuggled closer, and tipped her head back. "I haven't been this comfortable in a long time."

"Me either," he replied as he combed his fingers through her hair. Her eyes slid closed, and it was seconds before she was breathing evenly. Yep, this could work. He liked the feel of her in his arms, and he especially liked being *in* her arms.

He'd been walking through life in a fog, desperate to guard himself against anything that could hurt him further. In the process, he'd built a cage for himself, and he was tired of living in that dark corner. If nothing else, she'd taught him that it was better to feel life's arrows than drift through life numb.

The sinking feeling he'd had about the condition of his heart when he left this park was turning out to be right. He was leaving this blasted park in shambles and there wasn't a thing he could do to change it, nor did he want to.

17

The sun was barely peeking above the horizon when Riley woke up. Jax had held her while they watched the sunset, and she didn't even remember falling asleep, much less Jax carrying her to the tent. All she remembered was being in his arms and feeling warm, safe, and comfortable. Three things she'd never felt with another man.

Since she'd woken up first, it seemed like a good idea to try her hand at fishing again. If she had her way, they'd be eating well before striking out on the trail again. Fish weren't exactly a breakfast food, but she knew it was infinitely better than the puny protein bars they'd brought with them. If they were even half as good as they were the night before, it'd be a feast fit for a guy like Jax.

After digging for some bait, she worked through

the steps he'd taught her, baiting her hook and then casting her line out, giggling to herself when it sailed and then dropped in the middle of the creek. In her head, the crowd was definitely going wild.

The previous night's attempt was a horrible disaster. He'd made it look so effortless. Just flick, soar, and splash. He'd pulled in the first fish in just minutes, and then tried to help her. He'd been so patient too. Way more than her dad or Charlie. At least her dad was just easily frustrated instead of impatient *and* cruel. Eventually, she'd given up, and left the catching to Jax.

When they'd finished eating, she'd watched him, staring blankly at the fire, lost in thought. He'd fidgeted with his dad's letter over and over, grief and anguish swirling around him like ribbons twisting together. She'd wanted so much to take it from him, and not because he'd saved her. He was good and kind. If anyone deserved good things it was him.

A yank on the line pulled her from her thoughts and she nearly danced with excitement. The line yanked even harder, and this time she knew the hook was set. She reeled it in with giddy anticipation just like he'd taught her.

Her excitement turned to dejection when a large branch broke the surface. She'd done everything the way he'd taught her, and she'd still caught nothing? She'd wanted to catch enough that they could feast, so he could see that she was listening and that she had value. That she wasn't useless.

Frustrated with herself, she grabbed the handful of worms she'd dug up and stalked down the bank of the creek in a huff until she reached a spot that looked a little deeper. She baited the hook again, stepped closer to the edge, and cast the line. Surely, something had to be biting. Over and over, she cast her line and each time it was either a branch or something had snagged her bait and taken off with it.

Riley Vance had struck again. Finally, nearly in tears, she began her return to the camp. The funk clinging to her seemed to grow until she realized she'd been walking a little too long.

Of course, she'd gone further than she'd thought, and Jax was now waking up, wondering where she'd gone. If he didn't dump her right then and there, it'd be a miracle. Her only consolation was that she'd managed to stick close to the creek which meant she'd eventually make it back to him.

She rounded a small bend in the creek and Jax came into view loaded down with all of their gear, his eyebrows knitted together and his lips in a tight line. Yep, she deserved whatever ire was about to come her way.

He crossed the remainder of the distance between them, stopped, put the gear down, and set his hands on his hips. "You went fishing?" The barked question came out more like a harsh accusation.

Hanging her head, she replied, "I woke up, and I thought I'd catch breakfast." She bit back the tears threatening to spill and dropped the fishing pole. "I wanted to show you that I was listening. That I could be useful. That I was worth having around. When I didn't catch anything, I went further down, hoping I could find a better spot. I...I'm sorry. I should've—"

Before she could finish the sentence he had her in his arms, crushing her to him. "I'm sorry. There was no reason to be so gruff or raise my voice."

No reason? There was every reason possible, and now, she felt even more wretched that he was the one apologizing to her. They'd been chased across three states, and she hadn't even had the decency to leave him a note. "I made you worry, and I didn't even catch anything." Tears streaked down her cheeks. "You have every right to be furious with me for being so stupid, selfish, and irresponsible."

Leaning back, he tipped her chin up and brushed her tears away with his thumb. "You were trying to do something nice, and I had no right to yell at you. I can be upset without raising my voice or being harsh. You didn't deserve that."

She hugged him around the neck. "You dropped everything to help me. I should have left a note."

He rubbed her back and spoke softly, "Riley, I know you were trying hard to learn, and you are most definitely not useless. You have immeasurable value to me whether you can drive or fish or leave notes." When she didn't respond, he leaned back, coaxing her to look at him. "Hey, really, it's okay. I promise." He smiled.

Oh, this man. Kind and gracious and everything a woman could want. As their eyes locked, she could almost picture the house, the white picket fence, and a life filled with happiness. Not that there wouldn't be hard times, but problems seemed much more manageable when she was holding his hand.

Boy did she ever want to kiss him. Not just kiss him, but smother him in kisses. What she wouldn't give to be the one who could cup his heart and keep it safe from harm.

Holding his gaze, she palmed the side of his face and touched her lips to his and held them there a heartbeat before leaning back. "I—"

The sentence died as he brushed his lips across her and he let out a shuddering breath before sweeping them across hers again. Goosebumps lined her arms and raced to her toes as the air charged around them.

Again and again, he brushed his lips across hers in a maddening tease until he caught her lips in his teeth and coaxed her lips to part. He deepened the kiss, and she melted against him with a soft moan. In that moment, she knew she was ruined.

Their lips moved together and all she could think was that she'd never want a man more than she wanted Jax Kelly. She couldn't hold onto him tight enough or long enough to fill the need she had for him. With every second that passed, the ribbon tying her soul to his grew stronger.

With a groan, he broke the kiss and set his forehead against hers while they gasped for air. "We should probably get going." The words were punctuated with deep breaths.

In the back of her mind, it made sense, and she could see the logic, but that was the last thing she wanted to do. "Probably," she said as she began trailing kisses from his temple to his jaw, working her way back to his mouth. Each time he tried to capture her lips, she'd hover just out of reach.

The tease continued until a groan ripped from his throat as he slid his hand into her hair and cupped the back of her head. Not a breath passed until he was crushing her lips to his, igniting another fiery, toe-curling kiss.

When he broke the kiss again, she had no idea how long they'd stood there. All she knew was that her lips were bruised in the most delightful way, and her head was spinning from lack of oxygen.

"Now we really should get moving," he said, still breathing heavily.

As much as she hated it, she knew he was right since she had no idea how long they'd been standing there. The sound of underbrush and dead wood snapping in the distance cleared whatever haze was left from kissing him.

He gently set her feet on the ground and put a finger to his mouth. She nodded in understanding. Another snap and her heart slammed against her ribs even harder. He had his firearm, but that didn't mean the bad guys wouldn't have a gun too. The thought of losing him gutted her.

He looked around and his gaze landed to her right. She turned, following his line of sight and found a small grouping of trees with enough cover that it'd keep her hidden. He pointed to it and motioned to her to go.

No way. Shaking her head, she frowned. If they'd been found, it'd be nothing to hurt him and quickly find her. What would be the point in hiding?

He mouthed the word *yes*. When she didn't move, he mouthed *now*.

She pinched her lips together and shook her head again.

Jax's shoulders rounded as he held her gaze and he gave her the biggest, saddest puppy dog eyes she'd ever witnessed. Rude. How was she supposed to say no?

Fine. She grumbled to herself as she quietly crossed the distance and hid, looking for a branch or something to use as a weapon. If nothing else, she'd fly out of the bushes like a rabid honey badger and use the element of surprise to take down whatever bad guy happened to show.

Riley had tumbled down whatever mountain she'd been climbing and straight into the arms of a man she could see spending the rest of her life with. Yeah, it was important to get that flash drive to the authorities, but it was also important to keep Jax safe. If she didn't, her heart would be in pieces so tiny, it'd be impossible to put back together.

18

*J*ax could kick himself. He'd gotten caught up in kissing Riley and let his guard down. They'd stayed in one place too long and there was no telling who he might be facing off with. If something happened to her because he was distracted, it'd ruin him.

It'd been a fantastic kiss though, and it'd shaken him. He couldn't remember being so lost in someone that the world faded away. Kissing her was mind-melting, and he wasn't losing himself like that again until they were literally out of the woods.

When he'd woken up, and she wasn't there, his heart had dropped to his stomach. Then he'd realized the fishing rod was gone too. He'd quickly packed up and gone to find her. As he walked the bank of the creek, all he could do was picture Galen's men finding her and hurting her. The second she'd come into view, his heart had lodged in his throat and he'd never been so happy to see someone in his life. Then anger flared. She'd scared him.

She'd hung her head as she explained why she'd left the campsite and the anguish in her voice was heartbreaking. He'd picked her up, relieved that she was safe and feeling horrible for making her cry. Then *she'd* apologized and he'd felt like scum. She'd tried to do something sweet for him, and he'd thrown it back in her face.

One minute he was trying to reassure her that everything was okay, and the next he was kissing her. Well, to be fair, she'd kissed him first and whatever resolve he'd mustered to resist the temptation to kiss her had evaporated. The next thing he knew, he was kissing her, and heaven help him, he wasn't sure he'd ever get enough of her.

More underbrush continued to snap as footfalls grew closer. He checked where Riley was hiding making sure she was out of sight, reached behind him, and wrapped his fingers around the grip of the 9mm holstered snug against his back, hoping he didn't have to use it. Best case scenario, someone had stumbled onto the spot like he and Riley had. Worst case...well, he'd tackle that if he was forced to.

A moment later, a heavy-set man with a hat, cargo

shorts and t-shirt came into view with an equally heavy-set woman with a coat tied around her waist. As far as menacing threats, he rated them zero on a scale of one to ten and at the same time, something was off, like their appearances were a façade.

Although, his heightened paranoia could possibly account for that feeling, but they rubbed him the wrong way. He could see bumbling down a path, but what were the odds that they'd chosen the same direction that he and Rilley had?

"Oh, hey man, we're sorry," the guy said. "We heard the stream and wanted to check it out. We didn't mean to roll up on you." The man's gaze flicked to Riley's hiding spot.

The movement was so slight, had Jax not been alert, he would have missed it. His hand tightened around the grip of his gun. "No problem. I did the same thing."

The woman smiled as she scanned the area. "I can't blame you. It's so pretty and tranquil here."

"Yeah, it is. I've enjoyed it so far," Jax replied, tension building like he was playing a game of chicken.

The couple exchanged glances. "Well, we're not planning on staying long, so we'll get going. Again, sorry for the interruption." The woman smiled as she turned, and they headed back the way they'd come.

After the couple were out of view and their footsteps could no longer be heard, Jax let out a long breath and raked his hand through his hair. Riley peeked out from her hiding place and then walked to him.

"That couple gave me the creeps," she said.

"I didn't like them either." He huffed. "And next time, don't argue with me."

She sank her fingers into his t-shirt near the collar and brought him down eye-level with her. "The next time, you're coming with me or I'm not moving. I told you I wasn't going to leave you."

Man, he liked this feisty side of her, but her safety came first. He covered her hands with his and held her gaze. "My job is to protect you. I can't let anything happen to you, and hiding was the only solution I could think of. If something happens to you that I could have prevented, I'll never forgive myself." Just the thought of something happening to her made him sick to his stomach.

"And if something happens to you because you're protecting me, I'll feel the same way." The way her eyes were searching his made him swallow hard. "Together or not at all. Do you understand me?"

He couldn't help but smile. "What are you going to do if I don't?"

She narrowed her eyes as she pointed her face up at him, pressing her lips into a thin line. "I might be small, but you'd be surprised by the things I can do when I put my mind to it."

His head fell back as he laughed. "You're very cute."

"And mighty, so don't test me."

With a chuckle, he straightened and set his hands on his hips. "How are these people finding us? We're in the middle of a national park, and off the trail. It doesn't make sense."

"What do we do now?" she asked.

That was a great question. One he'd love to have an answer to. He took a deep breath and let it out slowly, trying to figure out their next move. He almost wished he hadn't suggested the park, but knowing the Beetle wouldn't have made it any further, the park was better than being stranded out in the open. This way, they at least had somewhat of a chance.

He rubbed his mouth with his hands. "I don't know."

The car was done. He wasn't sure why Noah hadn't been waiting for them at the entrance, and since he hadn't, they were now forced to hike to the tower because that's where Jax had told Noah to meet them. If the vibe he got from that couple was correct, he had a new challenge of keeping him and Riley safe long enough to actually make it to the tower.

"Let's get packed up and get some distance."

Once they'd gathered their things, they headed for the trail they'd used the day before. As they reached the edge of the tree line, he stopped and used his arm to hold Riley back.

That vibe he'd had held true. The couple was now joined by two other, younger men, and it appeared to Jax that they were in an animated discussion, a heated one at that as red faced as one of the two men were, giving the impression that he was the one in charge of the whole thing.

He put his fingers to his lips and then leaned in, putting his mouth against her ear. "That couple is talking to two men. They're standing in the middle of the trail."

"Now what do we do?"

"We stay off the trail and follow the creek." And quickly, too, since now it was abundantly clear that they were being followed into the belly of the park.

Straightening, he caught her gaze, and she nodded before tangling her fingers in his.

For the next few hours, they stayed close to the creek bank, following it until Riley began having trouble keeping up. When Jax found a good spot to rest, he set his pack down, and lifted hers from her shoulders. Until then, he hadn't really paid that much attention to it.

He tilted his head as he looked at the brand stitched

into it; one he didn't recognize. "Uh, where'd you get this bookbag? Is this Galen's brand or something?"

She took a seat and used her shirt to wipe the sweat from her face. "No, my best guess is that he used some printer who makes company uniforms or something. Mr. White gave it to me when I started working for him. It was basically the only bag allowed in the building for security reasons," she said and shrugged. "At least that's what he told me."

He looked the bag over, scrutinizing it. It looked innocuous, but Galen White hadn't avoided prison because he was stupid.

"After I tossed my phone, I thought I was safe, but they kept finding me. The only thing that made sense was the bag, but I dug in every pocket and when I didn't find anything, I figured it was because I was being careless or something."

Taking a seat next to her. "Would it offend you if I checked it out?"

"No, go ahead."

He ran his hands down over the entire exterior of the bag, coming up empty. There were no weird little pockets or anything that looked out of the ordinary. As he reached the *GW* stitched into the front, he picked at it with his fingers. His breath caught, and Riley perked up.

"Did you find something?" she asked.

"There's a circuit board behind the stitching."

She stared at Jax a moment before her eyes widened and her mouth slowly dropped open as realization hit. "That's how they've been…"

"If I had to wager a guess, I'd say these are given to all his employees so he can keep tabs on them. You wander too close to a police station…his people get an alert. You aren't the only employee to find something and go to the authorities. This man hasn't remained free because he was stupid and sloppy."

Her bottom lip trembled. "I'm so stupid. Why didn't I think—"

Putting his arm around her, he tugged her to him. "No, you aren't. I've seen a lot of devices used for tracking and the clever places they've been hidden, and I've never seen anything this sophisticated."

"I just feel so dumb." She rubbed her eyes with her hands.

"Then I'm dumb too because I didn't figure it out either." He touched his lips to her forehead. "Let's get your stuff out of it and send his men on a wild goose chase." He pulled his bag over and quickly rearranged things to make space for the few belongings she'd brought. "You can put your stuff in here, okay?"

She grabbed her backpack, unzipped it, and transferred her things. "Okay, so what's this wild goose chase idea?"

They needed the people who were looking for them to think Riley was still using the bookbag. That meant it needed to appear like it was still moving. He eyed the creek a second and smiled. "I have an idea."

Less than ten minutes later, they'd constructed a makeshift raft using branches and fishing line sufficient enough that it was capable of carrying the bookbag and handling the current without tipping over.

"Care to do the honors?" asked Jax, handing her the raft with the bookbag fastened to it.

With a nod, she took it from him, set it in the water, and pushed it off. "Maybe now we can have a moment of peace."

He would have agreed if it weren't for the fact that they'd stayed in one spot too long. Once Galen realized they'd found the tracking device, he'd be sending an army for them. He pulled the park's map out of the side pocket of his bag, opened it, and his gaze landed on his dad's handwriting.

A rush of air escaped his lips as it hit him that they would be stranded on the side of the road somewhere were the events in his life any different. His heart ached at the loss and soared at the realization that bumps, potholes, and rough terrain had led him to a woman he could see spending his life loving.

"Got a plan?" she asked.

He swallowed back the wave of emotion, nodding. "Uh, working on it."

People had left him, but if he just shifted a fraction, he could see it as an invisible hand, sending them on their way, so that he could be where he needed to be at the right time he needed to be there.

All the rough roads, potholes, and ditches that came before the forks were things that he'd needed to experience in order to take the best road. Without those, he may have chosen a different path and the experiences wouldn't have been what he needed to help other people. Maybe the hard things he'd been through were points in time he could handle where others wouldn't have been able to, and it was those experiences that led to a richer, fuller life than what he would have had if all his roads were smooth.

Whatever that letter contained, he'd face it. If it broke his heart, he'd use it, grow from it, and then use the experience to make a difference in someone else's life.

19

Oh, how Riley longed for the Beetle's metal seats. They'd only been walking a couple of hours, but her feet ached to the point she was tempted to apologize for being so mean to the car. She wasn't going to complain though. It was her fault they were in the predicament in the first place.

That stupid bookbag. Stupid, useless her. She smacked her toe into a rock like she was trying to hit Jupiter. It plunked into the water and made a squirrel look at her funny.

Galen White. His thugs. All the trouble and grief they'd given her. All because of that bookbag and her idiocy. Ohhhh, she was so mad her blood was boiling. The handful of gray clouds rolling in seemed to punctuate just how ticked she was at herself.

Jax didn't have to blame her, she had enough

condemnation of herself to make up for his part. Why hadn't she thought of looking behind that stitching? Or at the very least, remembered that Galen was the one who'd given it to her and tossed it whether she could find anything or not. As many times as his men had found her, it should have been a no-brainer once her phone was gone. She was such an idiot.

"Uh, Riley?"

She'd been so caught up in chastising herself, she'd powered down the trail and she was several feet ahead of him. As short as she was, and as long as his legs were, that was nearly a circus-performer-level feat.

He jogged to catch up. "It's not your fault."

"Yes, it is. They found me over and over after I dumped my phone." She was pouting and she knew it. Maybe even being a little irrational. Or a lot. "They even found me at the airport for crying out loud."

"You heard Mia. With as many cameras as there are in the airport, the fact that you evaded them as long as you did was a miracle."

"But I didn't learn about the hackers until after being caught at the airport. I should have clued in long before that…" Her gaze dipped to the ground and the word *useless* screamed even louder.

Tipping her face up with his finger, he smiled. "And if you had, I wouldn't have met you."

"And been chased, shot at, hounded, missed your conference, upended your entire life—" She threw up her hands, put her back to him, and crossed her arms over her chest. This whole thing was her fault, and the one sweet man who'd kept her safe was forced to deal with things he wasn't ready to deal with. All because of her.

He walked around her and faced her. "All worth it."

"How can you say that?" she asked and scoffed as she motioned to all the gear he was carrying. "I'm not even pulling my weight." Sure, she'd tried to carry some after sending her backpack down the creek, but he'd reasoned that they needed to get moving and they'd redistribute the weight once they made camp for the night. "I can't catch fish. I can't drive. I'm thoughtless and, and—"

"Brave, insightful, witty, and gorgeous."

Four words that would easily describe him way better than her. "Stop that. You can't be nice to me right now."

A few hikers passed by, smiling. Once they were out of earshot, he took her hands in his. "Riley, I was nearly one hundred percent sure you were in trouble when I asked you to lunch. I knew what I was doing when I did it, and I knew after talking to Noah just what we were up against. Not once have I regretted meeting you or anything else. If I had it to do all over again, I'd still choose you."

Pulling away, she hung her head and sighed as she closed her eyes. How was he so blind to all her faults? "I just…I just can't figure out why though. Charlie always told me I was useless and stupid. I mean, look at my parents. My siblings. What do I have to show for myself? I'm twenty-eight years old with zero accomplishments. I've done nothing of worth at all. Seriously, I can't. Even. Drive." Her frustration grew as she spit out each word.

He took her face in his hands, and hot embarrassment pooled in her stomach as she realized she'd said all that stuff aloud. Now she wasn't just stupid and useless, she was pathetic. She needed a hole or a portal or something that she could crawl into.

"Look at me."

She hesitated a breath and opened her eyes to find him staring into hers with an intensity that made her gulp. "You are not useless or stupid. You've faced obstacles and continued to climb your mountains. That's a lot more than most would do."

If she spoke, there'd be no way she could continue to bite back the tears threatening to spill.

"I see a woman who worked hard to get into nursing school, then had to quit because she lost her job. She didn't give up. She kept looking for a job and had plans to re-enroll in school. Then she found something evil, and she was so brave that she acted without even considering the danger she was putting herself in, and even after she understood, continued to put herself in harm's way. You're a cape away from a superhero in my book."

Great. Now he *was* going to make her ugly cry. "And it's sweet, but—" She pulled away and shook her head.

"You have an incredible heart. You're loyal, selfless, and kind. Those qualities are worth far greater than whatever accomplishments you think you need." He shifted until he caught her gaze again and smiled. "Charlie isn't worth a single tear if he couldn't see the diamond that you are, staring him in the face."

With the way he was looking at her, and the level of conviction in his voice, she knew he wasn't just trying to make her feel better. "You think all those things?"

"I know all those things, and those qualities will make you one of the best nurses to ever grace a hospital." He cupped her cheek. "I like you just the way you are, and I'm speaking from experience when I say that you're wonderful."

Her boat was nearly capsized, and there he was with a bucket, rescuing her once again. If she was wonderful, then Webster truly lacked a word to adequately describe him.

Tears welled in her eyes. It'd been a long time since someone made her feel like she was worth knowing. She hugged him around the waist. "That was the sweetest, most beautiful thing anyone has ever said to me." She leaned back and caught his gaze. "Thank you."

He leaned down, set his cheek against hers, and whispered, "If I was given the opportunity to go back and rewrite my history, I'd make the same decisions because they led me to you." When he pulled back, he kissed her nose and smiled. "You are worth every bump and pothole. Every single one."

Gulp. Her heart hurt that he'd gone through what he had, but even a slight deviation could have taken him from her, and the thought wrecked her. The word *fallen* was officially scratched out and the word *love* took its place. Oh, she loved him.

That little four-letter word felt infinitely larger as it floated through her mind. It was true though. She loved him. She loved how he looked at her. How he treated her. His bravery and selflessness. If anyone deserved hero status, it was him.

For now, she'd hold it close to her chest. There was a very good chance he was right about witness protection. If she admitted aloud that she loved him, she wouldn't be strong enough to leave. Everyone she cared about would be in danger, including him.

He touched his lips to her forehead and laced his fingers in hers. "Let's get moving. I think the reason you had so much trouble fishing this morning was because the water was a little too warm. Once it cools off, they'll move out of the deeper water and their hiding holes and bite better."

"Really? You think so?"

"Yeah, I do. We'll also look for a shaded spot, so that we're kept cool too."

She tilted her head as she looked at him. She'd clearly missed something while she threw her tantrum. His essence was different—lighter, peaceful. "Something's changed."

His lips quirked in a playful smile and his eyes narrowed. "How do you do that?"

"I should have noticed sooner, but I was fit to be tied." Her cheeks burned and she flattened her hands against her face to cool them. "I don't know how it works. I'll just get tingles, or my skin will itch. In high school, it wasn't so awesome because I was an odd, nerdy girl and the only time anyone liked it was when it worked for them. I got used a lot."

"I hate that for you."

She waved him off. "We were kids and I've come to appreciate it as I've gotten older. That's the reason I didn't give the detective the flash drive. Something was off, and I just couldn't."

"Does it always work?"

Shaking her head, she replied, "No. Obviously, when I'm distracted or upset it doesn't work."

"Weren't you distracted when you went to the police department?"

"No, I didn't realize who Galen was at the time. I knew he had connections and rubbed elbows with Houston politicians and others in the upper echelons, but I didn't know that his reach was so wide." She glanced at him. "The desk sergeant led me to a detective's office, and the guy was taking down everything I said, and when I mentioned Galen's name, it felt like the air was sucked out of the room. He made my skin itch, and I just couldn't shake the feeling that he wasn't trustworthy."

"When did you realize Galen was after you? Did you just sense it?"

"I wish." She chuckled. "I left the police department and went to my apartment building. When I got there, two men were loitering around the entrance, and I'd watched enough television to know that they weren't selling cookies. I got close enough and overheard them talking about me."

He pulled them to a stop. "Do you realize how incredible you are? To have so much awareness that you were able to take that drive and stay just ahead of them? There aren't many who could do what you did."

Looking away, she tried to fight a smile breaking out on her lips. "Whatever. Anyone else could have done the same thing."

"That isn't true, and you know it." He lifted her hand to his lips and kissed the back of it. "You are a special woman, and I'm going to keep saying it until you believe it."

Whew. He was making her tingle all over and not in the sensing danger sort of way. If he wasn't holding her hand, she'd be floating away. The way he spoke about her. The way he made her feel.

"It's your turn to spill." She pointed her face up at him and was once again struck by the sparkle in his eye and the way his countenance seemed to glow. "Now, talk." She'd be glued to every word too. Something profound had happened, and she was desperate to know what.

20

ax began walking again, fingers still twined in Riley's. Something had changed. It felt like his soul had been pressure washed. The only reason she had managed to get so far ahead of him was that he was lost in his own thoughts, reeling from the impact that a shift in perspective had given him. Hindsight was twenty-twenty, and he'd just put on new glasses.

And it'd all started when he met her. Anyone unable to see her value was blind. She hadn't just changed his plans. She'd changed his life, and absolutely for the better.

"I've been looking at the bumps and potholes wrong. I was so caught up looking at all the bad things that I missed the good things that came out of them. I've taken the good for granted. Really, I've got a great life with good friends and a job I love. Had any one thing been different, I wouldn't have met you. I wouldn't change that for anything in the world."

He pulled them to a stop and pulled out his dad's letter. "I'm ready and want to know what's in it, but I'm not sure I'll be able to keep it steady enough to read it. I was hoping…I was hoping you'd read it to me."

Her lips parted in a gasp. "Are you sure?"

"Positive." He smiled. "If I'm sharing it with anyone, it'll be you."

She took the letter and opened it as they began walking again.

"To my best friend and my boy,

"I don't know if you'll ever see this, but if you do, I hope it will help you understand why I left, and just how much you were loved.

"By the time you entered the world, your mom and I had settled into a nice, quiet routine of enjoying a typical family life.

"What you never knew was that we were skilled locksmiths. Specifically lock-pickers, but not your everyday pop-a-lock service, and not even the garden variety rob-a-convenience-store type. Our clients were black-market collectors that would hire us to crack safes for them. Before we became Scott and Vega Kelly, we were Clint and Doris Beale. And we were criminals."

Riley paused and looked at Jax.

His heart revved into third gear. "Keep going," he said just above a whisper.

"When we found out your mom was pregnant, that wasn't the life we wanted for you. People weren't allowed to just leave that world. So we changed our names and laid low.

"We thought we'd pulled it off until a previous client came looking for us. It was either meet him or risk exposing ourselves—and you. So we tried to thread the needle. You may not remember, but we took a long weekend for our wedding anniversary. We—"

He sucked in a sharp breath. "I do remember that. It was the same year my mom died and he left." Blinking, he shook his head. "Keep going."

"Do you want to read it from here?" she asked.

Shaking his head, he replied, "No, I'm not sure I have enough air in my lungs to read it.

"The client needed one of us for a large job that would take roughly a month to plan and execute. Your mom was better at cracking this particular type of safe, so to protect our identities and keep you safe, she agreed to do the job while I returned home to take care of you. We both knew the risks, but we didn't see any other way.

"A month later, I learned that something went wrong, and she'd died during the heist. I told you she left because holding a funeral would have meant exposing you to the world we'd worked so hard to hide you from."

Riley grabbed her water canteen, took a big sip, and clipped it back to her pack before continuing. "The moment your mom was killed, you were no longer safe. The life we'd left was colliding with the one we'd built. I left you that day because I knew my days of being Scott Kelly were over.

"Maybe there was a better way, but at the time, my heart was broken because I'd lost the love of my life, and you were all I had left of her. The risk of those people finding out about you was too great.

"I followed you, though. Valedictorian in high school and college, Navy officer, and doctor. You were a light in our lives, and you've made the world a better place.

"If you're reading this, it means I'm gone, and you're finally safe. I hope you can forgive me. If you can't, I'll understand. Just know that your mom and I loved you beyond words and it killed me to walk away.

"Take the items in this storage unit and do with them what you will. If you manage to ever forgive me, maybe think of me when you use the pickup and the camper.

"I love you and there hasn't been a day that passed that I haven't missed you.

"Love, Dad."

Jax stopped abruptly and raked his hands through his hair. He'd never been so blindsided in his life. "I… I…" He caught Riley's gaze. "I don't know how to process this."

She gently folded the letter, placed it back in the envelope, closed the distance between them, and hugged him tightly around his chest.

They didn't have time to be standing around, but his world had just tilted. His mom and dad were criminals, and they'd changed their entire lives so they could raise him. They loved him. His dad had left to protect him. If his dad had stayed…he couldn't even picture what his world would look like.

Riley set her chin against his chest, looking up at him. "Are you okay?"

"Honestly, I don't know. I mean, this changes everything." He palmed his forehead.

When he'd asked Riley to read the letter, he'd been bracing himself for something less life-altering. He'd had a new perspective, and he'd been prepared for right hooks and gut punches, but not…that. Not two people who loved him so much that they sacrificed themselves for him.

"Do you need to sit down for a second?" she asked, handing the letter back to him.

Shaking his head, he took it and put it back in his pocket. Yeah, he was in shock, but he'd made a promise to get her to safety. "No, we need to keep going. There are at least four people looking for us, maybe more. I wouldn't be surprised if they've already figured out what we did with the bookbag."

Silence fell over them as they began walking again. In five days, his world had been rocked, shaken, and stirred. He'd gone from being so angry with his dad that he wanted nothing to do with him or the stuff he'd left behind to seeing struggles as more than just the hard knocks of life.

His mom had kissed him goodbye the day before they left on their trip. When his dad returned home, he'd told Jax that she'd had an emergency thing at work and that she'd be home soon. He'd never even questioned why she didn't call him while she was gone. A month later, Jax was told she was gone and not coming back. It'd felt like she was there one minute and gone the next.

The man Jax knew was now reconciled with the man who'd dropped him off with the babysitter and never returned. It had to be so hard to learn that his wife was gone. Not just gone, killed. They'd worked so hard to leave that life behind, and it'd come knocking and destroyed everything. More than once he'd caught his dad crying, but Jax thought it was because he'd run her off and he felt guilty. In reality, he was grieving the love of his life.

Jax glanced at Riley, picturing himself in the same position as his dad. What if something happened to her? He'd known her less than a week and was in love with her. But he hadn't even built a life with her yet, and she could be yanked away from him. The thought made him ache.

"I can't imagine what my dad was going through to find out his wife had been killed." He rubbed his face with his hands. "How hard was it for him to hold it together and take care of me? I was angry Mom left, and I'd been taking it out on him."

"You were just a kid, and as much as he loved you, he understood that."

"He sacrificed everything, including me, to keep me safe." His voice caught and he shuddered. "All this time. All this time, I've held such contempt for him, and it was undeserved."

She took his hand and made him stop. "Jax, you were a kid. You didn't know the whole story, and what he told you was all you knew. Yes, he sacrificed himself, but that's what you do when you love someone, especially when you think they might get hurt. When you love someone, you cup your hand around their heart, hold it tight against your own, and fight their battles when they can't. Love is messy and hard. If it was easy, it would be worth nothing."

Before he could respond, a noise whirled in the distance. "Do you hear that?"

She stood quiet for a moment and then jerked her gaze to his. "Dogs?"

"Yeah. It could be innocent. People do go missing at times. I can see a sense of urgency since the longer someone is lost, the harder they are to find, but the timing is a little..."

"Suspicious?"

He nodded. That was exactly what he was thinking. "Yeah, we need to assume they're looking for us."

"What do we do?"

Just as he went to respond, a large droplet of water hit the top of his head. He scanned the sky, and his stomach dropped. Eerie dark clouds had rolled in, making the sky look like it was about to take its temper out on the earth. "That looks pretty bad and it's coming in fast." A loud crack of lightning laced through the sky, punctuated by a large clap of thunder, startling them both.

There was no way he could get the tent up in time. "We need to find shelter, now," he said. "If this thing drops enough rain, we could be looking at flooding." He took her hand, and they began running. "I'll look to the left. You look to the right."

"Wait!" She dug her heels in and took the chain from around her neck. "This needs to be kept dry."

Once it was in something watertight and secure, he took her hand again, and just as they started to sprint, the sky opened. In minutes, they were drenched, and the ground was soggy with visibility near zero. He jerked to a stop as her hand slipped from his and cursed under his breath. She'd stumbled face-first into a bare patch of dirt that was now a muddy puddle.

He closed the distance, yelling so he could be heard over the thunder and lightning, "I'm so sorry! Are you okay?"

"Yeah, but I can't see," she yelled back.

Scanning the area, he quickly found her glasses and handed them to her. "Visibility is bad, but we need shelter."

He tangled his fingers with her again and jogged at a pace she could keep. Finally, he spotted a large lean-to and guided her to it.

Once inside, he dropped his pack onto the ground and wiped his face off. Riley's hair was matted to her head, and her clothes were mud-caked. He'd missed the scrapes on her chin and the palms of her hands. On top of that, she was shaking so hard that her teeth were chattering.

They'd gained enough altitude that the air was colder and the rain even more so. He had to get her warm now.

Leaning down, he took her face in his hands. Hazy, unfocused eyes met his. "I'm going to turn around so you can change, okay?"

Her head bobbled like a dashboard doll, and it took her a second to register what he'd said. He turned his back to her and smiled as his gaze landed on a neatly stacked pile of dry wood. He said a silent thank you to whoever was gracious enough to leave it, and when she tugged on his shirt he turned around.

Hugging herself, her teeth clacked together. "Y-y-your turn."

Jax shook his head. "We need to get a fire going first so you can start warming up."

Once it was going, she splayed her hands in front of it, still shaking. "Fire good." She chuckled.

He took her hands and turned them palm side up. "I need to treat these."

"It's j…just scr…scr…scrapes." Her teeth clicked together as she shuttered. "Y-y-you need dry clothes too."

He wasn't cold, but she was right. "Okay, I'll be quick and then I'll treat them."

Closing her eyes, she nodded. "Okay."

Moving as fast as he could, he changed into dry clothes. "I'm done." He dug in his bag and found the first-aid kit. He crossed the tiny distance and kneeled in front of her, looking at her chin. "Well, you don't need stitches."

"Th-th-that's good."

He applied some antibiotic ointment to her chin and then moved to her hands. Pieces of dirt and splinters littered her hands and he carefully cleaned them before spreading ointment on them and bandaging them. "Are you hurt anywhere else?"

She put her hands up to the fire. "My-my-my knees, but it's o-o-okay. J-j-just bruises really."

"Let me see them."

"N-n-no that's okay."

He smiled as it hit him why she wasn't wanting him to look at her knees.

"I'm a doctor, remember?"

She hugged herself tighter and looked at the ground. "I j-j-just feel gr-gr-gross."

He ran his hand over her hair. "Hey, I know, but I've seen worse things than hairy legs, I promise." Leaning down, he caught her gaze. "It's okay. I promise that I'll find you just as sexy when I'm done."

"W-w-well, I d-d-don't have to w-w-worry about

fa-fa-freezing to death. I'm ga-going to die of embar-bar-essment."

Chuckling, he checked her knees, applying a little ointment to them. Her pants had kept them from getting scraped as badly as her hands and chin. He gently pulled the cuffs of her sweatpants back down. Even with the fire, she was still visibly shaking. Clearly, that wasn't working.

He rolled out a sleeping bag, unzipped it, and then pulled his shirt off before picking her up and getting in the sleeping bag, tucking her hands against his chest. He sucked in a sharp breath as her icicles disguised as hands touched his skin.

Tugging her closer, he ran his hands up and down her back, working to get her blood circulating. Finally, after what felt like forever, she slowly stopped shaking and sighed.

As the storm raged, all he could think was that this was the most comfortable he'd been in a long time. Her in his arms, breathing softly. This was something he could set on repeat for the rest of his life and never get tired of it.

"Jax?" she whispered.

"Yeah, are you okay?"

"I am now." A short pause. "Thank you."

He dropped a kiss on the top of her head. "Get some sleep."

She snuggled even closer if it was possible. "Did you call me sexy?"

His cheeks hurt he was smiling so wide. "Uh, yes, I did."

A longer pause. "It's not fair for Mr. McDreamy to hit an unsuspecting woman with that word. We're in the middle of the woods and we don't have a defibrillator." The words came out a little slurred.

"Uh, who?"

Something between a moan and a sigh poured from her. "You're an extremely good-looking doctor."

He held in a bark of laughter. "I think you should probably get some sleep."

"Jax?"

He rolled his lips in, grinning. "Yes?"

She took a deep breath, moaning as she let it out. "Best. Pillow. Ever."

"Goodnight, Riley."

Not a heartbeat later, she was breathing evenly. He pushed her hair back from her face and his gaze roamed over her. Falling for her had been so easy. Just a blink and she was all he wanted. At this point, he couldn't picture a moment in his life when he wouldn't want her standing next to him.

And she was most likely going into witness protection. Now he had to figure out a way to keep her, if at all possible.

21

*H*appy, warm, and content. Riley couldn't think of three better words to describe how she felt. As she shifted, her eyes popped open, and she realized three things all at once: Jax was shirtless with his arm draped over her waist, her hands were bandaged, and her body was smooshed against his in enough places that little wildfires were breaking out over her skin.

All she remembered was falling and then being cold. Beyond that, her recollection was muddled. Not that waking up with Jax was bad in any way. In fact, she'd be satisfied waking up like this every day for the rest of her life. Her curiosity, though, was centered around the decisions that had led her to her current state. There was also the nagging feeling that something seriously embarrassing had occurred. Which, knowing herself as she did, was less a question of *if* and more of just how mortified she'd be.

Tilting her head up, she inhaled deeply, and her eyes roamed over his face. He was her definition of downright beautiful. Add his incredible heart and sweet nature, it made him a top contender for the cover of GQ.

"Why are you staring at me?" His voice was husky.

She startled and quickly recovered. "I told you," she said, and then cupped her hand over her mouth. Killing her knight in shining armor with morning breath seemed a lame way to go. "Because you're cute."

His eyes opened and he flashed that sultry smile she liked so much. "What are you doing?"

"Morning breath."

He took his arm from around her waist and mirrored her. "Sorry."

She tilted her head down, hugging him around the chest. "Thank you for taking care of me. The last thing I remember is changing clothes. That's twice you've rescued me. I'm starting to think I need to offer you a punch card."

That letter his dad left was still a shock to her. High-end thieves, who'd given up a life of crime to raise their son? It was something out of a movie. His parents had loved him, and they'd done everything they could to protect him. She'd known there was no way he was at fault for his dad leaving him, even if Jax was a complete terror after being told his mom left. The letter confirmed it.

It didn't surprise her one bit that his dad had followed Jax through his life. After making the hard choices to keep his son safe, he would have wanted to keep watch over him. It was sweet, and proof that Jax was loved by his dad.

Jax laughed, and it rippled through her body. "I don't mind." He yawned and stretched what little he could in the sleeping bag. "As much as I hate it, we probably need to get moving."

Sunlight was just beginning to cast shadows inside the shelter which meant it wasn't *that* late. She groaned and snuggled closer.

He unzipped the bag and groaned as cool air rushed in.

On second thought. "Nope. Hard pass."

"Aren't you from North Dakota? It's not like it's a tropical oasis there."

Yes, that was true, but she'd grown accustomed to Houston's weather. What she liked most was how warm it was. Grumbling, she reluctantly rolled to her back, carefully pushed off the ground, and stood. Yawning, she stopped just outside the shelter and stretched. "Oh, I'm sore." Sore all over. Every muscle in her body seemed to be screaming at her.

Although she didn't recall the fall being all that severe, her body had a wildly different opinion. Her chin and knees were mildly sore, while her hands, when she moved them, were slightly painful, making it evident that they had taken the brunt of the impact. She delicately rolled up one of her sweatpants legs to examine her knees. They were bruised and tender to the touch, but not all that bad.

Jax joined her outside as he pulled a t-shirt over his head. "Could I look at your hands?"

She shoved her pant leg down and faced him. "Sure," she said.

He removed the bandages and his lips turned down as his fingers ghosted over her torn skin. "I'm sorry. I should have paid more attention."

Smiling, she replied, "They're just scratches. It's not that big of a deal."

"Yeah, I know...still..." He walked inside the shelter, returned with the ointment, and gently applied it to her wounds before bandaging them. "When we stop, I'll change them if it's needed."

She touched the underside of her chin and tilted her head back. "This doesn't feel as bad as my hands."

"It's not. Your hands took most of the impact of the

fall." He spread a tiny bit of the salve onto her chin. "Now, let me see your knees."

Her eyes widened. Her knees? It'd been days since she'd had the opportunity to shave her legs. All they needed was a little more time and they'd blend in with the forest. It was not happening. "Nope. They're sore, but they're okay."

A grin played on his lips. "You do remember I looked at them last night, right?"

Fire. Her face was on fire and there would never be enough water to put it out. Shaking her head, she replied, "Uh, no. I remember being cold and changing clothes, but that's about it."

"Well, I did, so there's no reason to be shy now."

Yeah, right. She dropped her hands to her sides and leveled her eyes at him. "Oh, yes there is. Unlike last night, I'll know, and I'll die."

Rolling his eyes, he sighed. "I'm a doctor. Believe me, there's not much I haven't seen."

"Yeah, well, you won't be seeing my knees again, at least not while I'm conscious or coherent." Her irrational response meter was pinging well off the scale.

"Riley, come on." He motioned with his hands for her to lift her pant legs. When she refused, he chuckled. "Really. I told you last night that I'd find you just as sexy when I'm done."

Oh, dear heavens. If this kept up, she'd spontaneously burst into flames. Sexy? A word that had never left the lips of a man in her direction. "I don't remember that."

"Well, I did." He gave a heavy sigh. "Seriously, though, let me see them. It's my fault you fell."

"No, it's not. At any point, I could have said something. Bad things happen, and that's just part of life. So, stop that." She paused a beat and added, "And the answer is still no."

His eyes narrowed. "I'll happily stop." He shot her a half smile. "As soon as you let me see your knees."

They stood there and faced off until she huffed and pulled her pant legs up. "See? They're fine."

Squatting down, he said, "Well, I wouldn't exactly say fine. They're bruised, but not as bad as I anticipated." He lifted his gaze to hers and then stood. "If you need more breaks today, let me know."

"I will." She shoved the legs of her pants down, ignoring the hint of pain as her hand briefly touched her left knee. By the time they made camp that evening, they were going to be miraculously healed.

Jax scanned the sky. "We're up pretty early, so even if we make frequent stops, we should be able to cross a lot of ground."

"I don't hear any dogs. Do you think they're still out there?"

Nodding, he replied, "Yeah I doubt they've given

up. I think the only reason we don't hear them is because it rained pretty hard and slowed them down, and while the rain may have dispersed our smell it didn't get rid of it. A well-trained dog will be able to pick it up and lead them to us. Which means if we stand around, they'll find us."

Sheesh. Talk about motivation to move. They'd got everything packed and began making tracks. This time, he'd put things together in a way that she could shoulder some of the weight of the gear.

Instead of fishing, they'd munched on some protein bars Jax had brought from the storage unit. Disgusting didn't begin to cover the horror that befell her tongue. She'd forced it down though just because she knew she needed it. It made her want to cry that they hadn't stopped at a gas station and purchased some food prior to arriving at the park. Although, had they done so, they may not have made it to the park at all.

As the sun moved higher in the sky, the more humid and warmer it grew. How had it gone from chilly to so humid it felt like she was walking through water? "I think I need a second," she said, breathing hard.

While they weren't officially on a trail, they'd been walking parallel to the one leading to the fire tower, and they'd hit a steep incline. She was huffing and puffing like she'd never walked up a mountain before.

So far, she loved camping as long as it meant not hiking. That she could do without.

"Okay. It's probably a good time to stop anyway. We can eat while we rest." As they looked for a spot to rest, the sound of a helicopter flying overhead caught their attention. "I can't tell which way it's coming," she said, watching the sky.

"Me either." He quickly stepped from under the cover of the foliage, turned in place, and stopped a second. He ducked back under and pursed his lips. "No identifying markers, but there are scenic helicopter companies in this area. It could have been one of them."

Her skin tingled and itched. It might have been a chartered helicopter ride, but that's not the feeling she got. "I don't think so. First the dogs and now that?"

"Exactly, and we know Galen is capable of anything. He's motivated, too." When the helicopter was no longer in view, he let out a breath, shaking his head. "I really hate not being able to trust anyone."

Nodding, she said, "Do you think they saw us?"

"There's no way to tell, but erring on the side of caution seems wise."

"What do we do now?" She wasn't sure if she wanted to know the answer. Her feet hurt, and she was tired.

He seemed to debate a second and then exhaled.

"Let's do what we planned. We'll rest here a moment, treat your hands, and then move on."

They wandered through the brush for a moment and found freshly downed trees. The storm must have been bad because one of them was completely uprooted. It made her wonder just how much rain they got and the potential for landslides. She saw enough video shorts to know that was a possibility in mountainous areas.

She shrugged off her pack and took a seat on one of the trees. Without thinking about it, she braced her hands against it and quickly pulled away, shaking them out. She needed to remember *not* to do that again.

"Did you hurt yourself?" he asked and tipped his head at her hands. "We need to put ointment on them, but I thought I'd wait until after we ate to rebandage them." He glanced skyward. "I'd planned on maybe foraging for a few edible plants, but seeing that helicopter, I don't think we should stay here that long."

Which meant another protein bar. *Gag.* Whoever packaged them, calling them delightful, clearly had no concept of the word. Just the thought made her stomach shrink back in terror like something out of *Psycho.* It'd be a lie to say she wasn't hungry though.

Digging in his pack, he said, "I know these are awful, but with the amount of walking we're doing we need the calories. It's easy to get run-down without realizing it. I'm sorry my plan changed."

"It's okay. Not like we can control the helicopters."

He opened his and bit off a chunk, and by the look on his face, he was choking it down.

At least she wasn't alone in her assessment of them. In her desperate attempt to eat hers, she bit off a huge chunk and shuddered as she forced it down. "Oh, these are awful. What sort of monster created these things?" She'd hoped she was hungry enough that they would taste better, but even as famished as she was, it wasn't happening. If anything, they were worse.

Much like herself, he forced down the rest of his bar. Then he pulled out the ointment and bandages. Once he had her hands treated and rebandaged, they were off again, making sure they stayed out of sight from anything that might fly overhead.

They settled into a comfortable pace and equally comfortable silence. Birds, frogs, and a host of other animals were singing as a creek roared like background music. Even with all that going on, it was still rather peaceful.

She wasn't sure she'd ever be a full-fledged, gung-ho camper, but if Jax was in the picture, she'd certainly try. *If* being the operative word.

More and more, she disliked the idea of going into witness protection. It felt unfair. She'd found the man of her dreams, and because of that jerk Galen, she'd have to give him up? There had to be a way to keep him.

Jax stopped abruptly, the movement burrowing through her thoughts and bringing her to the present. "Do you hear that?"

She strained and then looked at him. He'd been right. "Dogs?"

"Dogs." His eyebrows knitted together. "And growing closer." He turned his back to her. "There's bear spray in the bottom right pocket. It's the only thing in there."

Without responding, she grabbed the small canister and handed it to him.

"Walk ahead of me. I'm going to spray this as I walk backwards. It should help throw them off, but we'll need to do something long term to keep them thrown off."

Her knowledge of search and rescue dogs was limited to what she'd read on the internet and seen on movies and television shows. Well trained, they weren't misdirected easily, so finding something that would keep them confused was going to prove difficult. Hopefully, Jax's time with the Guardian Group had taught him something that would work. Otherwise, their trek to the fire tower just turned desperate and daunting.

22

"*I*t's been hours since I've heard the dogs," Jax said, scrubbing his face.

They'd found a patch of mud and smeared some of it all over themselves in hopes they'd confuse the dogs enough that they couldn't track them as easily. There was a possibility it worked, but also the team using the dog could've realized where Jax and Riley were going and stopped the search because they weren't needed any longer. Either way, they'd make it to the tower before the end of the day, and they'd need to be careful just in case Galen's men were waiting to ambush them.

Nodding, Riley said, "Maybe." The weariness in her voice made him stop short. "I can't say I've been keeping track."

There was no denying he felt as tired as she sounded. He'd kept track of the sun throughout the day, and if he had to guess, it was mid-afternoon which meant, for not being on the trail, they'd made decent time, especially since they weren't on the beaten path and they'd made it past the steep incline which was the worst part of the trek.

"Let's stop. We really don't have much further to go." He slid his pack off and nearly dropped onto the ground with his back against the tree trunk. "I'm not sure I could take another step at the moment anyway."

A long groan poured out of her as she stopped next to him and shucked off her gear. "Oh, I can't tell you how grateful I am to stop."

"I needed the break, so I figured you did too."

Stretching her arms over her head, she groaned again, letting them drop to her sides as she rolled her neck one way and then the other. She flopped down beside him, panting. "I'm going to need more than a minute. I feel like a wet noodle."

He put his arm around and tugged her closer. "You did great today. How are your hands feeling?"

"They're okay." She flexed her wrists and touched the underside of her chin. "My hands hurt a little, but not as bad as this morning."

Jax covered his mouth with his free hand as he yawned. "I'll check them before we start walking again."

"I don't even want to think about moving. If I do, I may cry."

Pulling her over his lap, he squeezed her to him. "I might just join you." He chuckled.

She leaned her head against his chest. "How are you doing?"

That was a good question. "Honestly, I haven't even been thinking about it, but I think I'm okay. I want to know more about my parents, I do know that. When I get the chance, I'm going to ask Ryder and Mia if they can maybe find some information about them."

"Can't say I'm not just as curious." She braced her hand against his chest and pushed back to look at him. "You have to wonder what their lives were like before they had you. I can't even imagine it."

"Yeah, I know. It makes me wonder about my grandparents. My dad would talk about them, but I never met them. I wonder if it was because of the life they led or if he was just making them up."

Tilting her head, her eyebrows furrowed. "Maybe he talked about them because that was the only way for you to get to know them."

That was a good point. "Maybe. It would make sense. It's almost like they created their own witness protection. I'm sure they weren't able to contact anyone who previously knew them, including their parents."

"Exactly." She smiled. "I know they were criminals, but it's still kind of cool. Talk about a plot twist." She laughed.

"No kidding." He sighed. "I'd already decided that I was done living in the past, but it's still an odd sensation. For so long, I felt broken. I'm still not sure I completely measure up, especially since the guys I work with—"

"Are bodyguards, not doctors. I'm guessing the men you work with look a lot like Noah—a guy who could bench press a tank with his eyelashes."

Laughing hard, he shook his head. That was a new one he'd be telling Noah. "I guess."

She took his face in her hands. "You don't have their brawn or training, but you still flew into action. The men who were holding me in the airport were armed. You could have been killed and I'll bet everything I have that not once did you even think about that. There are very few people in this world with your level of courage, and somehow, I was lucky enough to meet you."

Jax sobered as she held his gaze.

Keeping one hand against his cheek, she ran a hand over his hair. "I'm not just saying that to stroke your ego or make you feel better either." She trailed her fingertips down his temple to his lips and traced them. "You're pretty special to me, Dr. Kelly."

Sliding his hand up her back, he buried it in her hair and brought her lips closer, brushing his lips across hers. He continued the light touches, staying just out of reach when she tried to kiss him and kept the tease going until a small moan escaped before catching her bottom lip in his teeth. The moment he deepened the kiss, another tiny moan escaped as she circled her arms around his neck and melted against him.

Their lips moved together in a hungry, passionate dance that spoke of forever and growing old together. Every time he kissed her, it felt like his open wounds were being healed, and while there would be scars, they weren't tender to the touch. They were just there to remind him that he'd more than survived. He could move on, build a life, and find more happiness than he could imagine.

He didn't care what he had to do to be with her, but he couldn't envision his life without her. At least not one worth living. The kiss slowly ended, and he ran his lips from her jaw, back up to her cheeks, and across her nose.

When he reached her lips again, he immediately deepened the kiss, taking his time to savor her. Soft, languid, unhurried and just as heady as the last. He loved the feel of her lips, the way she returned his kisses, how tightly she held onto him.

The kiss slowly ended, and he set his forehead

against hers, breathing hard. "I think we should rest a few more minutes and get going again. The rest of the hike should be relatively easy, and I don't know what's waiting for us at the tower."

She slid her arms around his neck, extending her fingers into his hair, holding onto him. "Okay." The word came out breathy. "Do you think Galen's men know where we're going?"

The sound of a dog's bark startled them, but he knew that bark belonged to Rufus which meant Ryder wasn't far behind.

A second later, he cleared his throat.

Jax winced. While on one hand their situation had just improved, he had a pretty good idea his ride to headquarters was going to be miserable. Not only was he going to be ribbed about his hair, but he'd just been caught kissing the client.

Sighing, Jax said, "Hello Ryder."

Riley jerked her attention to Ryder and scrambled to her feet.

"Riley, meet—"

"Introductions later. We need to move," Ryder yelled, waving for them to hurry. "Hendrix and Sawyer are holding the tower and we have a rendezvous with a helicopter."

Jax bolted to his feet, quickly pulled on his gear,

and handed Riley's pack to Ryder. "She doesn't need the weight slowing her down."

Ryder grabbed it and threw it around his shoulder. Jax took her hand, nearly pulling her off her feet as they ran with Rufus leading the way. Without slowing, Ryder touched the earpiece nestled in his ear. "Stay close. Hendrix says they've got at least four, maybe five advancing."

When they reached the fire tower, Ryder held out his arm, stopping them. Across the way, Sawyer stood at the door, his head sweeping back and forth, then nodding.

"When I say run," Ryder said, "Run. Don't stop until we get inside that building."

Jax turned to her. "Did you hear him?"

She nodded. "I heard him."

"No matter what, you stay between me and Ryder. If something happens, stick with Ryder. Am I clear?" Her eyebrows knitted together. "Don't argue," he barked, as he pulled his service weapon.

A second later, Sawyer hefted his rifle in their direction and Ryder waved for them to move. Gunfire erupted as they raced to the tower, bullets whizzing past them, two grazing Jax's thigh relatively close together. He emptied his gun as they flew up the steps and through the entrance, diving for cover.

Two windows were broken. Sawyer and Hendrix

were on opposite sides taking turns trading fire through broken windows that faced the east and west. Both men squatted down, taking cover using the stones making up the base of the building. "They were herding you in," Sawyer said.

Nodding, Ryder ducked down. "I radioed Walker, and he's about eight minutes out."

Jax stayed low as he shucked off his gear and returned his firearm to the holster. He shouldered the wall a few feet from Ryder and pulled Riley flush against him before sitting with his back against the stones. "Are you okay?"

For a second, she sat stunned and then slowly shook her head. "I'm not hurt, but to say I'm okay would be a stretch."

He set his gun next to him and took her face in his hands, raking his gaze over it and down her body. "But you're not hurt anywhere, are you?"

She shook her head. "I'm not hurt," she said, lunging for him. She wrapped her arms tightly around his neck and buried her face in his shoulder. Gunfire rang out again, and her little body trembled as she constricted her arms around him tighter.

It went eerily quiet, and Sawyer looked at Ryder. "I've got a weird feeling."

"Expect some groundfire," Ryder spoke into the earpiece. "We would have picked you up with the helicopter, but you weren't on the main trail. Rufus tracked you." He grunted a laugh. "Oh, and nice hair, man."

Hendrix laughed.

"Shut up," Jax said. He set his cheek against Riley's so he didn't have to yell. "Hey. Want to meet the jerks I talked about?"

Rufus trotted over and nuzzled her arm.

"Hey, Rufus is saying hello."

She slowly loosened her hold and turned, keeping her body snug against his.

"The blonde guy is Ryder. The one with all the tattoos is Hendrix," Jax said, and tipped his head to the third man, "and you already know his name."

Rufus nudged Riley's arm again and she relaxed enough to scratch the dog behind the ear. "Well, aren't you cute?"

The dog sat as his tongue lolled out of the side of his mouth. Jax ran his hand over the dog's head. "Thanks, bud."

"Why weren't you guys at the entrance to the park?" asked Jax.

Ryder looked at him. "We've had system attacks non-stop, and they're good. When you sent that text, we were in the middle of radio silence while we patched code and worked with a few gray hats that Mia knows. It took a couple of days, and when the system came back up, the text came through. We'd already missed you at the entrance." He smiled. "But, they won't be getting through anymore."

Riley looked around and said, "Why do you think they aren't shooting at us?"

Sawyer popped his head up, checking the area. "They've got more firepower inbound."

Ryder nodded. "We threw them a few misdirects. They were coming in from the north and we intercepted them by coming in faster from the east. When the helicopter gets here, we'll need to move fast."

Riley crawled off Jax, reached for the gear, and dug out the chain with the flash drive on it. "That's the drive."

Ryder took it and shook his head. "Mia said this is the hard drive."

"I didn't look through everything, but I think so. There's definitely enough on it to point to Galen and what he's been doing." Jax put his arm around her as she returned to his side and plastered herself against him. Her body was still shaking but at least she wasn't in shock yet.

The sound of a helicopter in the distance got their attention and Jax got to his knees in anticipation of its arrival.

"Come, Rufus," Ryder said. The dog stood and cantered to him. With a few snaps, Rufus was secured in his harness attached to Ryder.

Sawyer handed his rifle to Hendrix and motioned for Riley to come to him. "You get to ride with me, okay?"

The words were barely out as a hail of bullets pelted the building, shattering a couple of windows and spraying glass everywhere. Not a second later, another one shattered over Ryder's shoulder and he ducked, using his arm to shield himself from the flying shards. "Helicopter's hit. Losing fuel. We need to go!" He began motioning for them to hurry and get strapped in.

Jax's brain kicked into high gear. The chopper's time in the air was limited and body weight mattered. Hendrix was a better shot than Jax, and with all the gunfire, Sawyer would need cover to keep Riley safe. If he stayed, he could act as a distraction or decoy. If nothing else, they'd have to divide their attention between him and the others.

He was also pretty certain that he wouldn't be shot on sight. Most likely, they'd been ordered to bring him and Riley in alive. If Galen was anything like Tom Harrison, he'd want the satisfaction of killing them himself. With Riley managing to escape, Galen would know his only hope of recovering his hard drive was an exchange. Not that he'd let them live once the exchange was complete, but it was his best shot.

Moving faster than he ever thought possible Jax

took Riley by the arms and shoved her toward Sawyer. "Take her and get her out of here." Sawyer moved quickly to fasten the harness around her, tucking her hands against his chest. He took his rifle from Hendrix and nodded. "Secure and ready to go."

As the helicopter hovered overhead, Jax held up his arm to shield his face from the debris whipping around them as he moved over to Hendrix. "I need your service weapon." Hendrix's eyebrows furrowed. "You're a better shot. Sawyer needs cover."

Hendrix held his gaze a second, a silent understanding passing between them. He slowly nodded, pulled his handgun from a holster affixed to his hip, and pushed it into Jax's hand. "Stay alive. I can't make fun of your hair if you're dead."

Jax rolled his eyes. "If something happens, tell her I love her."

Hendrix nodded as three cords dropped to the deck circling the tower. Sawyer swung around, using his boot to clear the jagged pieces of glass from the window before stepping through it. Ryder and Hendrix followed and the three of them clipped the cords to their vests.

Gunfire erupted again and more windows shattered. Riley twisted around as they were hoisted off the deck, found Jax, and their eyes locked. He loved her, and he'd kept his promise.

23

*R*iley was beside herself. Of course, with the helicopter losing fuel, if they'd tried to go back, not only would they risk losing the hard drive, but their lives as well. As upset as she was, they'd made the best decision in the moment. When they landed so rough at a nearby airstrip, she'd known that was true. Had they flown even a bit further, they'd have crashed.

Everything had happened so fast. They went from sitting against a tree kissing to hiding inside the fire tower to being hoisted into a helicopter as bullets flew by and windows shattered. It was the most terrifying thing she'd ever experienced. Until she realized Jax wasn't with them.

As the helicopter landed, Noah and Mia jogged toward her, and Mia laid her arm across Riley's shoulder and led her inside the building into a stair-well and through the building into a bedroom.

They were barely a step inside when Riley wheeled around and faced Mia. "We need to go back and get Jax." Even as Riley said it, she knew it was more than just a simple U-turn. If Galen's men let him live, they'd offer him up as a trade and immediately double-cross them all.

Mia's eyebrows knitted together. "Believe me, we will do everything in our power to get him back. Okay?"

Riley covered her face with her hands, unable to hold back the tears.

Hugging her, Mia rubbed her back. "I know what you're going through because I've experienced it. You feel raked out and terrified and helpless. But you aren't." She held Riley out from her. "We will get him back."

"You have?" Riley took her hands from her face and fidgeted with her fingers.

"Yes, Noah was shot and decided to sneak out of a safe house and get caught by Tom Harrison so that I didn't have to look over my shoulder the rest of my life. While the situation may not be the same, the emotion is. You feel so helpless."

Well, she was right about that. Riley felt like a wet noodle. "They'll use him to try to trade, right?"

"That's what we're expecting. Galen will want that hard drive. It'll expose his network and put him in prison if he doesn't get it back. He's been shrewd and he's not likely to change his tactics when they've been so successful." Mia sighed. "Until we hear from him, all we can do is wait. I hate it, but there's really nothing else we can do. Why don't you get cleaned up while I make you something to eat. Then you can rest."

Riley grunted. "Not hardly."

Mia smiled. "I totally get it. I promise we won't keep anything from you so the moment we hear something, I'll come get you, okay?"

Nodding, Riley's shoulders rounded. "Okay."

As soon as the door shut behind Mia, Riley dissolved into tears again. Mia was right, but that didn't stop her from picturing Jax sitting by the door of the fire tower as she was lifted into the helicopter. What if that was the last time she saw him? What if she never got the opportunity to tell him she loved him? That it didn't matter how safe she was, it wouldn't be a life worth living if she wasn't with him. The thought made her sick.

She trudged to the bathroom, resigning herself to do what Mia suggested. If or when Galen contacted them, she wanted to be refreshed and alert and ready to go. Not that she thought she'd get much sleep, but some was better than none.

Three hours later, they'd heard nothing from Galen yet and she was a ball of nerves. It seemed like a long time for him to just let them squirm, but she suspected Galen had tried to get Jax to give up Guardian Group's location and failed. If she was right, it meant he needed to come up with a plan that resulted in both Riley and Jax dead.

Ryder and Mia had taken the precaution of building a Faraday cage—which was basically a protective cage for electronics to prevent outside interference—after she'd spoken to them the first time. Mia had the hunch that the hard drive would have some sort of security on it, and she'd been right.

Had they opened it like a normal thumb drive, it would have alerted Galen to their location, automatically uploaded the contents to a cloud service, and then immediately fried their systems.

Once they'd accessed it, they'd learned it was a massive, top-of-the-line, twelve terabyte drive with thousands of images, communications with influential people and politicians along with videos they were sure Galen used as blackmail. From the little they'd told her, Riley was glad she'd passed on the offer to sit in with them.

A knock came from the door, and she practically ran to it and whipped it open. "Please tell me he's okay."

Concern deepened the lines on Mia's face. "He's... alive." She tipped her head to her right. "Let's go to the conference room. We've got plans to make."

"Alive? Just alive? What does that mean? Is he hurt?"

Mia waved for her to come with her. "Come on."

"That doesn't answer my question." Yeah, she was begging, and she didn't care.

Mia gave her a weak smile. "I love him too. He's one of my closest friends, and I'm just as worried."

Riley lowered her gaze to the floor, furiously wiping away tears. "I'm sorry. I'm not—"

"It's okay. You're worried and frazzled and reasonably so. Now, let's take those emotions and funnel them into determination to get him back."

Lifting her gaze to Mia's, Riley caught her bottom lip in her teeth and nodded. They walked in silence until they reached a large room with a long conference table. As Mia and Riley walked into the room, tension filled the air, and it was obvious she wasn't the only one worried.

Noah sat at one end while Sawyer was to his right with Hendrix next to him. Now that she could see their faces, she wondered if it was a security firm or a modeling agency. Sawyer with his light blonde hair and sea green eyes was a sight to behold. He was massive and muscled too. Hendrix sported more tattoos than she'd ever seen on a person, and he was equally attractive. The gold band on his ring finger told her he was taken. She glanced at Sawyer's hand and found it bare, which surprised her with as attractive as he was.

Ryder, who struck her as a surfer more than a computer expert, sat to the left with an open laptop in front of him. Mia took a seat next to Ryder and motioned for Riley to take the seat next to her.

A large projection screen flickered to life with Galen's smug mug in perfect color. Knowing what she did, it made her feel naïve that she never saw how slimy he was when she first met him. Had she been so desperate for a good job that she just waved off the creep vibes he was giving off now? Noah nodded to Ryder and the video played.

"You have something I want, and I have something you want," Galen said. The camera swept right and zoomed in on Jax sitting in a chair with his chin on his chest.

Riley's vision tunneled as she stared at the screen. It had the feel of the warehouse where she worked which confused her. Why would Galen hold Jax hostage there when everyone knew where it was? It didn't make sense.

The camera zoomed in closer, and Riley's heart lodged in her throat. Swollen eyes, a busted lip, and heavy breathing sounds that indicated they'd done more than rough up his face. A man lifted Jax's head, smacked him on the cheek, and said, "Wake up!" before smacking him once again. Jax's eyes fluttered open and closed just as fast.

The camera returned to Galen. "As you can see, he's alive. If you'd like him to stay alive, you'll follow my directions and do exactly what I tell you to do." He smiled. "Lucky for you, you haven't accessed it yet because I'd know. You'll keep it that way too."

Now Riley was unbelievably grateful for Mia's hunch.

Galen came back into the frame. "Since I know how you operate, Mr. Wolf, we'll be doing things my way. I have a benefit gala that takes place in Houston the night after tomorrow. I haven't chosen a plus one yet, and Ms. Vance would be a lovely arm piece to accompany me."

Ew. That slimy, low-life, nasty jerk wanted to take Riley as his date?

He continued, "I've attached an invitation with this video that will allow her inside the building. You'll drop her off while I'm a safe distance away, and when I'm sure she's alone and has my hard drive, I'll arrive and tell you where the doctor is." He dropped the arrogance and leaned forward. "Make no mistake, I mean what I say. I've wired that hotel with explosives. You will follow my directions, or your doctor, along with twenty-eight hundred people, will die."

The video clicked off and Riley felt clobbered. No way was Galen letting Jax live no matter how well they followed his instructions.

"I'm going to work on finding out where that was shot."

Riley sat forward. "It's the warehouse where I worked, and it doesn't make sense. Why would he hold Jax there when we know where it is?"

Mia stood, walked to the front of the room, and returned with a laptop. "I'm going to get the blueprints to that hotel."

Sawyer held up a finger. "I've got buddies who do bomb detection, and I know we can trust them."

Noah nodded. "Do it, and once Mia gets the blueprints, she'll shoot them to you."

Hendrix rubbed his jaw with his hand. "Jax isn't going to be in that warehouse. It's a distraction. I'll bet money he's brought to the hotel. That way he doesn't have a body to deal with."

"Can you play the part where it looks like he's in an office?" Riley asked.

"Sure," Ryder said. A second later, the video played again.

"Stop!" Riley pointed to a picture frame to the left of Galen's head "That's my office. It makes no sense to keep Jax in a warehouse that I'm familiar with. I bet he's bringing Jax to the hotel, putting him in one of the rooms, and while we're going room to room, he's going to blow the hotel."

Everyone stared at her, and she shrank back a little. "I mean, I've watched a lot of action movie and it's really just a theory."

Noah shook his head. "It's a good theory."

"It's a great theory," Mia said. "I thought I'd check airstrips and jet schedules before grabbing the blueprints. He's got a private jet landing tomorrow evening. My bet is that he has that hotel wired and while we're trying to get everyone out, he'll try to skip the country."

Hendrix and Sawyer stood, and as they reached the door, Hendrix paused. "We'll get him back."

"How on earth will we find Jax going from room to room? The second he can, he's going to leave the hotel and blow everyone up." Panic built and pooled in her stomach.

Taking a deep breath, Noah sat quietly for a moment. "We need to catch Galen off guard, and I think I might have the perfect idea—"

"Don't!" Riley barked. "I don't want to know. I'm not sure I'd be able to hide it, and I don't want to jeopardize it." With as nervous as she was now, it was going to be even worse at the gala. Galen would know just by looking at her that something was off. She wasn't about to jeopardize the chance to catch him off guard.

Noah nodded. "All right. We'll take care of that on the way. Let's get moving."

Well, at least Riley knew Jax was alive. Whatever she had to do to find him and get him back, she was doing it. She would tell him she loved him, that she wanted to be with him, and then smother him in kisses.

24

*J*ax knew his name was being called, but whatever he'd been drugged with was powerful. He tried to lift his head and it felt like his neck was made of jello.

"I'd suspected we calculated your weight wrong. Guess I was right."

Jax fought the fog, and again tried to lift his head without success. Now, he had a pounding headache right behind his eyes and he was dizzy. He sat there a moment, eyes closed, trying to push away the grogginess.

"You need to wake up, so you can watch the show." The man smacked his cheek. "Come on, doctor. Wake up."

Shaking his head, he tried to clear the fog and regretted it. The last thing he remembered was waiting until he couldn't hear the helicopter any longer before surrendering to Galen's men. He'd held the gun up, and Galen's men had rushed him, and that was it. He'd been blindfolded and was almost certain he'd returned to Houston.

The next time he woke up, his hands were bound behind his back, and he was tied to a chair. In between demands for the location of Guardian Group headquarters, he'd been beaten. He was certain he had a few broken ribs and the rest weren't exactly great either. When they'd finally figured out he wasn't talking, they'd popped him on the side of the head and the lights went out.

He'd come to in a cell and shortly after, two men unlocked the cell, held him down and injected him with something. Most likely, they wanted to transport him without drawing attention to themselves. It was easier to stuff a knocked-out guy into something than someone who could potentially fight back.

During all that, he'd thought a lot about Riley and the future he wanted. He'd promised himself that the next time he saw her, he would tell her he loved her. He'd held in so much from his past and she'd helped him see things from a different perspective. It'd changed how he viewed his life and his past. He'd left Houston broken, or at least feeling broken, and he didn't see himself that way any longer.

Jax's vision cleared a little and a man stepped into view. "Who?" Blinking, he worked to clear the rest of the haze from his mind. The man was dressed in a tux with his dark hair combed back. Even dressed up, the guy felt slimy. "Galen White?"

"That's right." He sneered. "If your boss, Noah Wolf, and Miss Vance do what they're told, you might actually get to see them again."

Even groggy, he knew that was a lie. "We both know that isn't true."

Galen grunted. "I didn't say for how long." He straightened his cufflinks. "Your boss is used to dealing with idiots like Tom Harrison, but he's in for a surprise tonight. He's going to figure out Harrison is not some idiot who doesn't know what he's doing."

Grunting a laugh, Jax's head fell forward. That drug was kicking his keister, and he was feeling worse by the minute. "And my boss doesn't run the best private security company by letting scum like you outsmart him."

There was a snarl and then Galen's hand was around Jax's neck, squeezing it as he pressed back far enough that Jax wondered if the guy wasn't trying to snap his neck. With his face inches from Jax's, Galen's lips twisted. "You are in no position to talk about smarts. You should be grateful that you're still alive."

Jax struggled to breathe, and just as the edges of his

vision turned blurry, Galen released him, and he stepped back.

"I hope we have an understanding now." Galen's phone rang and put it to his ear.

No matter how hard Jax strained to hear what was being said, he couldn't. What he did know was the man was arrogant and easily angered. Alone, they were bad traits. Together they could be deadly. Maybe if Jax could get under his skin, he'd say or do something to give a clue as to what he was planning.

Galen slipped the phone back into his pocket. He stepped to the side and two monitors came into view, each with four different video feeds. "I had this prepared just for you. Now, you can watch as I stroll into the gala with Miss Vance as my date. Maybe if you're lucky, she'll find you before I blow the place. Or, maybe they'll follow directions, and you can have her when I'm done with her."

Red-hot anger flared and Jax fought against the cuffs. "If you touch her, I'll—"

"Do nothing." Galen walked to the door and opened it. One of the men from the airport stepped inside and sneered.

"If he tries anything, just shoot him."

The man nodded. "You got it, boss."

The door clicked shut, but it barely registered as Jax scanned the monitors until his gaze landed on one of the video feeds in the far-left corner of the left monitor. There Riley was in color in a royal blue dress with her hair swept up. She was gorgeous all the time, but man, she was stunning. And that creep was going to put his hands on her. He strained against the ropes.

"Stop. I still owe you for the airport so don't think I won't shoot you, orders or not."

Jax swallowed hard and pinned his gaze on the monitor.

25

*R*iley's stomach was in knots. Her knots had knots. Any minute, Galen White would be walking in the door, and she'd have to pretend to be nice to the jerk until she knew Jax was okay and where she could find him.

She fidgeted with the drive, rolling it between her fingers. It was so small and held such power. Hopefully, the power to put Galen behind bars and free his victims. It wasn't getting lost this time either. Using the Faraday cage, not only had Ryder copied Galen's drive to several other physical hard drives, but he'd also set it to be released to the public as soon as Jax was located and safe.

Of course, Galen was going to try to double-cross them. She'd known that before Noah even mentioned it. Noah had planned for them too with a series of contingencies should anything go south.

Walker had used a drone to survey the warehouse. Like most days, trucks were picking up as well as delivering. They'd known their theory about Jax being there was backed up when the drone picked up a faint heat signature in one of the loads. Walker had followed it to a downtown parking garage and they'd lost them after that. While they couldn't be positive Jax was being taken to the hotel, it did seem to line up with their hunch.

Sawyer's buddies had each checked into the hotel under the guise of a training conference being offered across the city and there being a mix up with their booked hotel. As far as Riley knew, they were currently combing the hotel with their dogs. She was unaware if they'd found anything yet. The hotel was large though, it took more than a few passes to make sure nothing was done during their last check. Overall, their plan was working and would continue to work.

As far as events went, if she wasn't absolutely terrified, she'd probably be enjoying herself. Mia had loaned her a dress that she'd used for a wedding, and with just a little adjustment, it'd fit perfectly. The soft blue, empire waist dress made her feel great. Her hair was pinned up, with a beaded clasp holding it in place. Silver strappy kitten heels completed the look. As she'd given herself one last glance, she'd wondered what Jax would think.

The event location was in one of the ritziest places she'd ever seen. None of the hotels she'd ever been in was as nice as this one. It reeked of fancy rich people who had personal hotel staff that would run their errands while they soaked in the hot tub.

"Miss Vance," Galen said as he set his hand on her elbow. "Walk with me."

She cut a glance at him. "Where is Jax?"

"Do what I tell you to do, and you'll see him soon enough." He smiled as the cameras flashed. "Now, walk."

When she tried to jerk her elbow away, his fingers dug into her skin and he leaned down, holding a toothy grin. "Do that again, and I'll give the order to have him shot."

Fear pooled in her stomach, and she worked to shake it off. Jax needed her and she couldn't afford to fall apart. "Fine."

He took her hand, hooked it through his arm, and straightened. "This is a benefit gala, and you're my date. Smile and act the part, Miss Vance."

She held her head high, smiling like she was channeling Miss Congeniality at a pageant.

"Good girl," he said. "When we get past all the photographers, I want you to hand me the hard drive."

"I'll hand you the hard drive when you tell me where Jax is," she spat back.

Galen dug his fingers into her skin again. "You'll do as I tell you."

Oh, she'd never wanted to claw someone's eyes out so bad in her life. She pinched her lips together and nearly growled in frustration.

"I said smile."

She did as she was told, pasting on her best smile while wishing he'd trip and fall on his face. They made it through the throng of photographers lining each side on the way into the room and she blinked trying to see. As many flashes that went off, it was a wonder she wasn't blind.

He turned to her, held out his hand, and smiled. "Hard drive."

She pointed her face up at him and glared. "Jax."

His eyes narrowed and he pulled out his phone, putting it to his ear. "Kill him."

Her eyes went wide, and she shook her head. "No." She fumbled with the necklace and pulled it over her head, shoving it into his hand. "Now where is he?"

The jerk's lips lifted in a snarl. "I still need a date. When I'm done with you, I'll tell you where he is, and you'll behave until then." They walked down the aisle and stopped at one of the banquet tables three rows from the stage.

He pulled out an electronic device the size of his hand and inserted the hard drive. A moment later, his phone rang. The conversation was brief, and when he returned his phone to his pocket, he slipped the necklace over his head, tucking it behind his white button-up. He pulled her chair out, and she paused a moment before taking her seat.

"Lucky for you, the hard drive passed the test," Galen said, pulling his chair closer to her before taking a seat.

Rolling her eyes, she crossed her arms over her chest and seethed as he blathered on about this and that while the room filled with those attendees. More than once, someone wandered over, shook his hand, and stroked his ego by telling him how thankful they were and appreciative of his time and donations.

If they only knew…

As the lights dimmed to a single spotlight, a woman with beautiful silver hair walked onto the stage, stopping at the podium. Noah had spoken about a previous member of Guardian Group helping them, but she'd had to decline. Riley was a little sad she wouldn't get to meet Pamela Williams. While it was sad how the group started, the way she'd honored her husband's memory was admirable.

The founder's husband was a detective who was killed in a drive-by shooting, and unbeknownst to her, he'd left her a sizable fortune. To honor his memory, she'd created the Guardian Group to help those who had nowhere else to go. It'd made the group all that more distinctive in Riley's mind.

"Good evening. I'm Pamela Carlisle. Some of you might know me as Pamala Williams. It's been a while since I've visited Houston, but when I was asked to officiate I couldn't say no." She smiled. "We're here to honor some of Houston's most generous donors. Without their financial contributions, many of the services available to our most vulnerable wouldn't be possible."

Applause erupted, and Riley wanted to throw up. This evil man sitting next to her deserved nothing except a sentencing to life in prison. She pinched the bridge of her nose, working to drown out the pomp and circumstance as a few awards were handed out.

Time was ticking by, and she was just sitting there while these people flapped their gums. She needed to find Jax. To make sure he was okay and tell him she loved him.

The woman set her hands on the podium and scanned the crowd as she spoke, "We have something special this year. One of our donors has gone above and beyond, dedicating his life and money to bringing awareness to domestic violence and child trafficking. Kind, generous, humble. He's done so much for

Houston and surrounding communities." She paused as the crowd gave applause. "The first person to receive this award…" She picked up an envelope and pulled out what looked like card stock. "Galen White."

For a second, it looked like Galen was stunned as a spotlight narrowed in on him. Just then an idea hit Riley that this was her chance. She smiled and slipped out of her chair, clapping a moment before bracing her hand against his chest. She snatched the hard drive and yanked, breaking the chain. "You'll tell me where Jax is right now, or I'm going to have the sound guy play all your greatest hits." She leaned back, smiled, and began clapping again.

His lips tightened in a thin line, and they faced off for a second before he leaned over. "Very top floor, last door on the right. Now give me that flash drive back."

She slammed it into his hand, took off running, and stopped once she busted through the double doors of the event room. The very top floor of the hotel. Last door on the right. "In a pig's eye," she whispered to herself.

Even stunned, Galen wasn't going to give her Jax's exact location. He was sending her on a hunt, so he had time to accept his award, make a small speech, and bolt to that jet he'd rented. Which meant she needed to hurry. She used her thumb to turn the small earpiece

Mia had given her with instructions to use it the moment she found Jax.

Riley closed her eyes and tried to put herself in Galen's shoes. Jax would have to be close by. It wouldn't even surprise her if he was sitting on top of the explosive.

The Houston Tunnels. The hotel she was in sat directly above one of them. She'd learned there were service entrances that many of the hotels and businesses connected to the tunnel. She took off at a run again, stopping near the public entrance from the hotel to the tunnel and looked around. A few feet away, she found an unmarked door with a keycard.

Fantastic.

She retreated as a man swiftly strode to the door, let himself in, and she quickly raced to slip her foot in before it slammed shut. As she counted to thirty in her head, she stretched out the earpiece and set it in her ear. "Mia?"

It crackled for a second and Mia's response was broken. "I'm…here."

"Service entrance below the hotel." The tunnel had to be messing with it. Riley repeated herself twice more, praying to whoever was listening that someone would find them. She cautiously entered and abruptly halted upon hearing voices coming from deeper inside the room.

Tiptoeing closer, she strained to hear what was being said.

"Boss said to stay here just in case one of those Guardian people figured out where we are. He said I was to shoot him if there was trouble." She recognized this voice as one of the men from the airport.

"I'm telling you boss just told me to come down. There was a new award handed out and he was the one they chose. He said something's fishy. Start the timer."

There was a pregnant pause. "Boss said he'd call."

Riley chanced a peek and watched the man from the airport dig into his pocket, pull out his phone, and hit a button before putting it to his ear. He took it away and looked at the screen. "No service."

"That's what I'm trying to say. Boss said to set the timer and get out." The thin guy in a hotel uniform checked his phone. "He should be done with the speech now. We need to get to the car."

As they turned in her direction, she looked around, found a laundry cart, and hid inside. She held her breath as they walked past and waited until the door slammed shut before jumping out.

She raced down the narrow aisle and nearly fell as she slid to a stop in front of Jax. Taking his face in her hands, she lifted his head until they were at eye level. His face was pale, and his skin was clammy. It broke her heart to see him hurt. His eyes were so swollen with his jaw bruised and lips busted.

"Jax?"

It almost seemed like a fight for him to open his eyes. "Riley?"

"Yeah, it's me. Are you okay?"

"No," he whispered. "They drugged me. I'm dizzy and nauseous. Hard to think."

Looking to her left, she found the bomb the two men spoke of, and her eyes widened as it counted. "We need to get out of here, okay? I'm going to untie you."

She gently placed his chin against his chest, quickly untied his legs, and rushed to untie his wrists. When she reached the knot holding him to the chair, she paused. If she just untied the rope, he was going to hit the concrete floor face-first. She ran back to the laundry cart, rolled it towards Jax and emptied it to soften his landing.

She undid the second knot, and he sprawled out on the pile of laundry. She rolled him over and took his face in her hands again. "Jax," she said and shook him. "Jax."

His eyes fluttered open, and she knew there was no way he was going anywhere. "Hey, when did you get here?"

"Just a moment ago."

His lips quirked up. "That's good. I need to…" He

inhaled and his eyebrows knitted together. "My head hurts."

Yeah, they'd whammied him with something. Knowing Galen and the type of things he did, it didn't take a leap to guess it was something nasty. She smiled and pressed a kiss to his forehead, wishing she could tell him she loved him and smothering him in kisses. As it stood, even if she told him, he wouldn't remember it and she certainly wasn't kissing him when he was this out of it. "You need to stay awake, okay?"

Her heart hit her stomach as he answered with a low moan and his eyes fluttered shut. He needed medical attention, and a bomb was sitting not two feet from her. Even if they did escape, what were the chances they'd escape the blast?

The door to the entrance jiggled, and she grabbed a mop leaning against the far wall. In her head, she knew she had no chance against a gun or any of Galen's thugs, but at least she could say she didn't go down without a fight.

It blew open with the distinct sound of a knob hitting the wall and bouncing off. She braced herself as she stood in front of Jax. Relief flooded her as a dog barked and Sawyer, along with a man she suspected, was one of the bomb disposal men he knew.

She dropped the mop and kneeled next to Jax. "They drugged him with something, and I'm guessing it's…" She couldn't say the words. Sawyer nodded. "Those drugs have a range of effects, and it's hitting him hard."

Swayer pulled a radio from his vest, relayed their location, and requested backup before squatting next to Jax, shaking him. "Hey." He shook him a little harder. "Hey, Jax. Hey, man, wake up. Hey! Jax."

"We need an ambulance."

Sawyer put the radio to his mouth. "We need immediate medical assistance. Jax is drugged with an unknown substance and unresponsive." He'd barely finished returning his radio to its holster when two more men walked past them to the bomb and began assisting the first guy. One of the men called over his shoulder. "Bomb is neutralized. We'll get in touch with the local squad."

"Thanks." Sawyer lifted his head, acknowledging what the man said and returned his focus to Jax. What bothered her most of all was the concern written on Sawyer's face. Riley couldn't imagine the things he's seen and if he was this worried…

Now, all they could do was wait. Wiping her eyes, she lifted a silent prayer that he'd be okay. The moment he was coherent enough to hear her and understand, she was telling him she loved him. She was picking him, and if he'd let her, she was planning on forever.

26

*J*ax peeled his eyes open and groaned. Well, as much as he could with two black eyes. He'd slowly gained consciousness and based on the smell and sounds; it was easy to guess he was in a hospital. Being the doctor was great. Being the patient not so much.

He shifted on the bed and sucked in a sharp breath. Every inch of his body was sore from being used as a punching bag. With the way his ribs were wrapped, he was right about a few of them either being broken or bruised.

The bed moved, and Riley braced her hand against the bed as she leaned over him. "Hey." Her smile came into focus and a glassy sheen coated her eyes.

"Hi," he croaked and worked his jaw. He was pretty sure there wasn't an inch of his body that wasn't bruised in some way. "My mouth has never been so dry."

A second later, she put a straw to his lips, and he drained the cup twice before pushing it away. The water left an icy trail all the way down.

Riley leaned over him again. "I can probably guess the answer, but how are you feeling?"

"Like a supercharged bus hit me." He let out a breath, grimacing as he shifted again, trying to get comfortable. "How long have I been here?"

"About two days. Galen used GHB on you, and it didn't play with your body chemistry."

That didn't surprise Jax. The last memory he had before he passed out was just how terrible he'd felt. "I'd say so. What happened? Did you go to that gala? I feel like I remember seeing you."

"I'm the one who found you. You were barely conscious. Sawyer wasn't far behind me, and his buddies disarmed the bomb—"

"Bomb?"

She nodded. "Yeah, it wasn't more than about a foot or two from you. Sawyer radioed for an ambulance, and they rushed to get you here. They treated you with activated charcoal and started an IV for dehydration."

He covered his mouth as he yawned. He couldn't tell which hurt worse, his jaw or his mouth. "I feel wiped out."

"I bet you do. When you're feeling better, I'll tell you the entire story, but for now, I'm just happy you're awake." She palmed the side of his face. "I was so worried. I..." A long sigh poured out of her and her eyes glistened. "Galen sent us a video of you, beaten and tied to a chair. For a moment there, I thought I'd lose you. He was arrested, by the way."

"Yeah?"

Nodding, she gave him a wide grin. "Very publicly. Every news agency was there, filming him as the police walked him out of the building, handcuffed. He's already had a bail hearing. He was a flight risk, so bail was denied."

"Good. The creep needs to stay in jail." He covered his mouth as he yawned again and blinked. "I think I want to stick with being a doctor. This action stuff isn't nearly as fun as it sounds."

Chuckling, Riley combed her fingers through his hair. "I think you need to rest some more. We can talk later."

He shook his head. "I promised myself that the next time I saw you, I'd tell you I love you. In my head, I could say it, but I..."

"Thought I'd go into witness protection?"

Nodding, he lowered his gaze. "Yeah, and it was stupid."

She took his chin in her fingers and lifted his gaze

to hers. "No, it wasn't."

Jax cupped her cheek, rubbing his thumb across it. "Yeah, it was. Those guys were whaling on me, and all I could think was that...I'd nearly let the past take everything from me. None of it mattered. No matter where you are, I love you. I don't want a future where you weren't in it."

Tears pooled in her eyes as she smiled. "I don't want a future where you aren't in it either. When I said we were in this together, I didn't realize it at the time, but I meant forever. I love you and you're the only one I want."

He pushed her hair back from her face, smiling. As happy as he was, he was exhausted and fighting to stay awake. "I love you, and while it might not seem like I'm jumping for joy, I am."

She softly touched her lips to his. "We're a team. I'll jump for both of us." Her lips quirked up. "I'll be here when you wake up. I love you with all my heart. I'd kiss you, but your lips are—"

He took her chin in his fingers, pressing his lips to hers. "It'll take a few years, but I'll make up for all the kisses as soon as I can." He smiled as wide as he could.

"I'll hold you to that."

As he drifted off, for the first time in his life, he had hope for the future. She loved him and he'd spend the rest of his life loving her.

EPILOGUE

Eight months later...

Jax pulled at his collar as he stood in front of the small gathering of friends and family. Any minute the wedding march would play, and Riley would walk in, no doubt gorgeous in her wedding dress. According to Mia and Hendrix's wife, Britney, she was going to make him cry.

Elbowing him, Hendrix leaned in. "You ready?"

"Been ready." Jax chuckled.

"I don't know if I could stand in front of so many people," Sawyer said, leaning over. "All of them staring at me."

Hendrix shook his head. "Nah. The second Riley walks in, Jax won't even know anyone else is here.

Britney was the most beautiful women I'd ever seen, and our wedding day put her in another solar system."

"If you say so." Sawyer laughed.

"I know so," Jax said, confident that Hendrix was right, especially since he'd attended that wedding and witnessed the man tear up.

In the last eight months, so much had happened. Galen was done. The hard drive was filled with evidence that would take years to process.

Ryder and Mia found as much information on his parents as they could. It'd been both eye-opening and life changing. Just like his dad said, they'd been expert thieves before they had him. No amount of digging into them led to any evidence connecting them to a crime. Had they wanted to, they could have had him and continued doing what they knew, but they'd chosen him. The only disappointing thing was finding out his grandparents had passed away almost a decade ago.

He'd spent a few months talking to Kennedy, and he'd closed that chapter of his life. Yeah, they'd been criminals, but the people he knew were good, honest, hard-working people who loved and doted on him. Jax had even come to terms with Mike's death and learned to appreciate their short friendship and the impact it had on Jax's life and choices.

After dating Riley for a little more than three months, he'd asked her to marry him. He knew he wanted her, and he'd spent so much of his life afraid to live that he wasn't going to waste one more second of it. He knew marriage was work, that relationships weren't always easy, but he also knew he was determined to make it work and she was too. Pledging his love and commitment for her in front of everyone was only a formality in his mind.

She'd re-enrolled in nursing school as soon as the next semester started, and they'd planned their wedding and honeymoon around her school break. Once she was finished with her degree, she had an open offer from Noah to join Guardian Group, assisting Jax.

Another elbow from Hendrix brought Jax to the present, and his pulse jumped as the wedding march began. As the doors to the church opened, his eyes locked with Riley's. It was her and him and nothing else. She was radiant in a simple satin gown that hugged her curves. Her hair had grown out to a little past her shoulders, but she'd pulled it up, leaving tendrils framing her face.

As she reached the front of the church, her dad kissed her cheek and eyed Jax. "You're the only man I'd trust with my little girl's heart and safety. I've called you son for months now, and I'm proud to make it official today, Jax. I couldn't be happier with the man she picked to be her husband."

Riley's family was massive, with grandparents, cousins, and aunts and uncles on both her mom and dad's side. It'd felt like he'd found the rest of his missing pieces when he met them. They'd quickly welcomed him with open arms, and he loved them. It almost seemed like they'd grown closer to Riley for his sake after learning about his parents.

"Thank you, sir...Pop."

The man smiled, Riley took his hand, and he'd never felt more confident a decision in his life.

As far as ceremonies went, they'd kept the wedding relatively simple. The minister spoke a few words about the significance of what their pledges of love would mean. He led them through the vows and the exchange of rings. Once they finished, the man clasped his hands in front of him and said, "I present Mr. and Mrs. Jax Kelly. You may kiss your bride."

He took her face in his hands and smiled. "I love you, and I will never stop."

She circled her arms around his neck. "I didn't know what the word meant until I met you. I love you."

Their lips touched, and the only surprise of the day

was how different this kiss felt. It was a promise of more than love and commitment. It was sealing the deal of spending the rest of their lives walking through life together no matter what it threw at them. They'd hold hands, weathering the storms.

For a list of all books by Bree Livingston, please visit her website at www.breelivingston.com.

ABOUT THE AUTHOR

Bree Livingston lives in the West Texas Panhandle with her husband, children, and cats. She'd have a dog, but they took a vote and the cats won. Not in numbers, but attitude. They wouldn't even debate. They just leveled their little beady eyes at her and that was all it took for her to nix getting a dog. Her hobbies include...nothing because she writes all the time.

She loves carbs, but the love ends there. No, that's not true. The love usually winds up on her hips which is why she loves writing romance. The love in the pages of her books are sweet and clean, and they definitely don't add pounds when you step on the scale. Unless of course, you're actually holding a Kindle while you're weighing. Put the Kindle down and try again. Also, the cookie because that could be the problem too. She knows from experience.

Join her mailing list to be the first to find out publishing news, contests, and more by going to her website at https://www.breelivingston.com.